MOMENT OF RECKONING

Sam'l reached a bit farther down the back of his neck than before and in one motion brought out a scaled-down version of a Green River knife that most mountain men used. It was his ace in the hole, and he put it to good use. In one motion he threw it into the guard's chest.

"Now, Finn!" Tom yelled, pushing Tally away as he brought his Dragoon around and shot the guard nearest him.

I pulled my own Dragoon out. I started shooting like there wasn't no tomorrow. If I hadn't, damn it, there wouldn't be no tomorrow!

People started coming out of everywhere just then. . . .

RIDING SHOTGUN

Jim Miller

FAWCETT GOLD MEDAL • NEW YORK

A Fawcett Gold Medal Book
Published by Ballantine Books

Copyright © 1985 by James L. Collins

Library of Congress Catalog Card Number: 84-91715

ISBN: 0-449-12484-3

Manufactured in the United States of America

First Edition: March 1985

To the P.E.N. Organization for all they've done for writers in this country . . . and to Christine Friedlander in particular, for being a part of it all.

Chapter 1

A bullet careened off the rock formation to our rear, striking the side of our freighting wagon, sending a splinter of wood flying up into Tom Dobie's cheek. They had us pinned and they knew it and so did we, but this wasn't any time to be shy about anything, and there were some things my partner wasn't shy about at all. No, sirree.

"—Damn it!" I heard him cuss as a volley followed the first shot, drowning out his voice. I was reloading and saw the vein in his neck bulge nearly to bursting as he brought his shotgun to his shoulder and let fly one barrel of buckshot to our front right, the second to our left, the two positions we were drawing fire from.

"I get my hands on one of them yahoos, he's gonna meet a slow death, Finn," Tom said through gritted teeth, replacing the shotgun with his own pistol, "a real *slow* death."

"You trying to kill 'em or just scare 'em?" I asked as more lead flew our way and more ricochets made it sound deadlier than it was. If we were going to get out of this alive, one of us had to keep his sense of humor, so I tried to make light of it. Tom was good with his shotgun, but it was useless at the range we were shooting in now. But then, maybe I'd have done the same if that splinter had gone flying into my face. Either way, Tom wasn't nothing but mad.

"Both!" He glanced at me in that way of his, from the

side of his face with one eye sticking out at you just enough
to let you know he's all business. Unless you got used to it,
it could make you right nervous, and right now gunfire was
doing a good enough job of that for me.

"Pard, this ain't a paying proposition," I said, taking in
the all of six feet that separated us and our wagon from the
highwaymen looking down our throats. A few more ricochets off the rocks and one or both of us was going to get
back shot a-purpose. And that, friend, is something no one
should have to look forward to.

"Only for them if we don't make it out alive," was all
Tom said.

"Give me some cover," I said, handing him the Colt revolving shotgun. "Maybe I can light a fire under 'em."
Tom frowned at first, then saw me glance to the far left and
knew what I had in mind.

"Just give me a clear shot at 'em."

I nodded and that was all the understanding either of us
needed right then. Tom brought the Colt's long gun over the
top of our wagon again as I ran past the rear wheel to a
smaller rock formation to our right. I felt sure I would catch
a slug then, but the dust kicking up at my heels and the thun-
derous roar of Tom firing two more rounds from the Colt
were the only disruptions I had as I made my sprint to cover.

This was the first time in six months that anyone had tried
to hold up our freighting business. I think Tom had expected
it to happen sooner or later as much as I had, although he
never said so, but then this was California in 1850 and the
gold rush had brought out the greed in more than one man
who'd come here looking to strike it rich. We'd gotten halfway to the assay office when these half dozen or so highwaymen threw down on us. Neither Tom nor I had been hit
so far, but if we didn't roust these birds from their nest up in
those rocks, we'd be more than just sitting ducks. We'd be
dead ducks.

I was within pistol range now and could see two of them
from my position. I was starting to form a plan in my mind
but never did get to finish it. Things started happening real

fast just then, and there was little time for thinking. The horses had gotten increasingly skittish in their harnesses as the gunfire rained down on us, and now they were trying to get out of the way. Not that I'd blame them, for I was as allergic to lead poisoning as anyone, man or beast, but when they moved it was Tom who was put in danger!

At first he tried to follow the wagon as it moved away from him, but I knew that wouldn't last long at all. Tom and I had fought together in the Mexican War a few years back, and I knew that when someone opened the ball, well, Tom was going to have his say about how the music was played. And that was just what he did now as he threw caution to the wind and stood dead still as the wagon moved on. I figured he had about two shots left in the Colt's shotgun before he had to start using his own pistol. That was when I snapped off three quick shots at those two buzzards I'd spotted, hitting both of them. By that time I had their attention and Tom was running to the left and tossing lead his own self. Within a matter of seconds we both had .44 bullets ricocheting inside that rock formation, giving the outlaws a taste of their own bitter medicine. I had about two shots left in my second Dragoon pistol when I thought I heard horses riding away. The gunfire died out, the only shot coming from Tom's side as I worked my way up to the two men I'd downed.

"They won't be bothering no one else," Tom said when we met at the top of the formation. The two men I had shot lay lifeless on the ground. "Recognize either of 'em?" he said, turning one over with the toe of his boot. I shook my head. "Me neither," he agreed.

The horses hadn't taken the wagon too far off, and we loaded the two dead men atop the ore we were carrying as though they were so much dead weight to be carried into town. If nothing else, I knew the sheriff would be interested in them.

"That was pretty good shooting, Finn," Tom said once we'd gotten back on the trail. He wasn't the kind to hand out compliments too freely, so when he did you knew he meant them.

"Just determination," I said, trying to smile. It gets kind of hard to do once you come as close as we had to losing our lives.

"How's that?"

"Well, hoss, we may be a two-man freighting business, but I figure we need all two of us to run it, so I reckon I was determined to keep you alive just then." It was true, for a small operation like ours had the same responsibilities as the bigger ones did; the only difference was that we didn't have anyone to delegate that responsibility to except each other.

Tom smiled. "Don't give me that." There was a mischievousness about him now, the way he got when he poked fun at a body. "If you was determined to get out of that fix back there, it was more to be around to meet the stage tomorrow when Tally gets here than to save my hide."

I didn't say much to that, for there was a lot of truth in what Tom was saying. I had an uneasy feeling in my stomach then. Not about the holdup, you understand. The way I was feeling I'd have rather gone through another gun battle without a complaint in the world. But maybe a man is supposed to feel like that when he's going to meet the woman he loves but hasn't seen in four years.

Tomorrow I'd know one way or another.

Sacramento City was the staging area for supplies and whatnot for the northern mining areas. It also had the nearest stagecoach station, and it was there Tally would be arriving. There were those who claimed that San Francisco, another fast-growing city on the coast, was the place to be, and from what I had heard that might be if you were in the gambling or shanghaiing business; but it was Sacramento that the miners looked to for the necessities of life these days. Bordering the Sacramento River and an inland waterway from Frisco, Sacramento supplied two of the larger mining towns in the territory, Marysville to the north, and Stockton to the south. It was also the end of the line if you were taking the Overland Trail on your westward trek. Of course, only those who could afford the prices of a coach ride from Saint Louis could make such a trip. If you waited around to eye them, like I did once, you'd discover that nearly every coach was full to overflowing with people and baggage, and the clientele that got out ran to doctors and lawyers and such. Not that I ever asked any of them why, you understand, but I'd never seen a dirt farmer or anyone else who'd just sold all his worldly goods for a pick and a pan dressed up near as spiffy as those gents that got off the stage.

Seeing it now as we rode in, I couldn't help but remember the hundreds of one-man tents and shanties that had made up the town when Tom and I first got there. Oh, there were some still to be seen on the edges of town, but for the most part the place was getting what my brother Nathan called ''right citified,'' meaning that there were two- and three-storied buildings that comprised the city's hotels and businesses, along with its gambling establishments and saloons. In a way I reckon I had my own sort of respect for those who had decided to make this town a permanent structure, for when building had begun not all of the cottonwoods had been cleared of the area. Many still interspersed the sides, backs, and fronts of the wooden buildings, giving the place a nice touch. Or maybe I had just spent too much time on the Texas plains and Mexican deserts *not* to appreciate the sight of trees.

Tom put the wagon around the side of the depot and left for the saloon to get a drink. But I was determined to be there when the stage came in and managed to get on Lisa's nerves in no more than ten minutes. As Tom's wife she was normally a patient woman.

''Finn,'' she said finally, ''go get a drink with Tom. The stage isn't due for another half an hour.'' Then, placing a hand on my arm, she spoke in a voice not much louder than a whisper. ''Relax. Everything's gonna be all right.''

Tom was seated at a table in the saloon with a burly-looking sort of fella who had somehow squeezed himself into one of those back east tweed suits that some of the businessmen were wearing. A shock of unruly hair stuck out from beneath the bowler hat he had pushed back on his head, and I found myself wondering if he hadn't at one time been a bouncer before going into whatever business he was in. Tom offered me a seat and yelled for another glass as the big man threw a ham-sized fist my way to shake.

"Hiram Johnstone," he said in a husky voice that was at the same time pleasant enough.

"Mr. Johnstone's from the Adams Express Company, Finn," Tom said, pouring me a drink. The way he said it sounded as if he were looking for some kind of reaction, although I wasn't sure just what it should be.

"Sort of out of your territory, aren't you, Mr. Johnstone?" I said, sipping my drink. "Seems to me your outfit's headquartered in San Francisco." I'd heard of the Adams Express Company before, but then, not many of us independents hadn't. Adams Express had originated in the east someplace and set up a headquarters in San Francisco in the winter of '49, not long after the first rush of gold seekers had arrived in the territory. They were big and used to having their way, and just knowing that gave me an idea of what it was Tom was looking for from me.

"Perhaps, sir," the big man said, "but Sacramento won't be out of the way for long. You see, I was just telling your friend here how much I'd give him for his freighting outfit, wagons, horses, and all."

"Mister, he's not only my friend," I said, "he's my partner."

"Claims to be shelling out *top dollar*," Tom said, with added emphasis on the last words. "Says he'll give me a couple, maybe three thousand dollars for our outfit."

Now, hoss, I don't often get what you call a look of astonishment crossing my face, but there must have been one there then, for I found myself looking at the man as if he were stark, raving mad!

"Mister, I put out more money than that just to get this outfit started!"

The pleasantness in Johnstone's face was gone now, replaced by a quick look of anger, the kind that shows up right quick when you run across people who are used to having their way and then don't get it.

"I wouldn't be too hasty or forceful, my friend," he said in a hard, even voice. "Everyone else I've spoken to is willing to sell to us. And we're quite large. You know what that means." He said it with the kind of overconfidence a man oughtn't have if he's going to survive in this land.

"Sure," I said, throwing back the rest of my drink as I got up from the table. "Just means you got that much further to fall when you do."

"Thanks for the drinks, pard," Tom said, finishing his own. "But you'll have to excuse us now, we've got a stage to meet."

I do believe the big man would have taken a chance on starting a fight right then and there if he hadn't seen Tom pick up his sawed-off scattergun, which he carried with him all the time. Seeing a piece like that tends to put a crimp in your style, no matter how tough you think you are.

"Here, he give me this," Tom said when we got outside, sticking what looked like a business card in my pocket. I pulled it out, glanced at it quickly, and pushed it back down in the pocket. "Says to get in touch with one of his agents if we decide to sell."

"Not hardly," I added as we headed for the depot. "We've been here just a tad longer than some fancy back east express company, and I figure we can outlast 'em. Besides, they charge more than we do to ship ore." After we'd walked a ways I found my curiosity getting the better of me as I glanced at Tom's shotgun. "Doesn't that thing bother Lisa at all? I mean—"

"Nope," he said with a sly smile, "just blowhards like that fella back there." He was silent a moment before adding, "You've got to remember, Finn, that there ain't a helluva lot of people who'll go up against sure death, or even slow death for that matter."

I knew what he meant, for that seemed to be what made the difference between some of the legends this country was producing and the rest of us mortals. Bowie and Crockett and Travis and Boone were growing in myth and legend. Hell, you could still find copies of the so-called adventures of Davy Crockett, supposedly penned by himself, throughout the country, but the man had been dead for some fourteen years now. Bowie and Crockett and the rest would charge hell with a bucket of water, put out the fire, and skate on the ice, while to your average man it most likely wasn't worth charging hell, since all he had was a thimble full of water. I reckon for most folks that makes all the difference when it comes to putting a label on heroics.

My thoughts returned to the present as the six-horse hitch of the stagecoach came thundering by us and Tom and I ran the remaining half block to the depot. Out of the corner of my eye I had caught a glimpse of the men atop the box as the coach sped by. The driver was leaning on his partner, his chest covered with blood, and it wasn't until I reached the halting coach that I realized I had my Colt in my hand. It was too late to do anything, but there are some habits a man gets into that are hard to break. Obviously, something had gone wrong on the trip, and I found myself saying a silent prayer for Tally's safety.

"What happened?!!" the depot manager yelled, charging through the office door as a crowd began to form.

"It was a pack of outlaws!" the man holding the reins said excitedly. "Twenty, thirty miles back. Ralph, here, got pretty bad shot up—"

"Get him inside, quick!" Suddenly, Lisa was in charge, giving orders to anyone standing nearby as Tom and I helped the wounded driver down off the box.

"Do I know you?" the manager asked, throwing a questioning glance at the other man, who must have been riding shotgun during the ride.

"No, likely not. They hired me out on the east side. I needed a ride back home."

"Well, you're fired!" the manager said. "Fill out a report on what happened, draw your pay, and git!"

"But I saved it!" the man yelled, but it was already too

late, for the manager had stepped back inside. In desperation
he turned to Tom and me, who seemed to be the only ones
left to listen to him. I was only giving him half an ear, however, for I was busy looking for Tally.

"See," the man said, pointing to a strapped-down strongbox atop the coach, "I brought it in! Tain't much of a
payroll, but I brought it in!"

"Well, what did they take?" Tom asked.

"I reckon they's just getting greedy these days and figuring the bigger trunks is got all they need."

I frowned, not sure of what he was talking about.

"You didn't have that kind of look on your face when I
saw you last." I turned toward the voice and briefly saw the
smile on Tally's face before she was in my arms kissing me.
"But you didn't forget how to kiss," she said when someone in the crowd let out a whistle and we parted. I gave the
fella a mad look and led Tally inside the depot.

She hadn't changed a bit, from what I'd seen so far. A tall
woman with graceful features and black hair to match her
eyes fit the description of the woman I'd left in New Orleans
so long ago, as well as the one who'd just gotten off the
stage. And now, just as then, she wore the fanciful clothes
of a woman bred to city life.

"That's it!" the man who'd brought in the stage said
from behind us, excitement again in his voice. "They took
her trunk! That's it!"

"Oh, be quiet, you old coot!" came another familiar
voice as Sam'l Dean followed us into the depot. He was Tally's older half-brother, and it didn't seem as if he had
changed either, still being as outspoken as he wanted to be
and not giving a damn what anyone thought of it. "That's
right, Finn, they taken Tally's trunk and thass it," he said.

I stuck out a hand, felt Dean's firm grip in mine.

"I'd watch who you call an old coot, hoss," I said
smiling. "You ain't too awful young your own self."

My comment gave the man who'd been riding shotgun
pause to laugh, and it was hearing that laugh that gave him
away. I knew I had seen him before, although I'd not had

time to place him what with all of the commotion and confusion taking place. But then, maybe it was because the fella had his hat pulled down over his face. When I pulled his hat back and saw his features I knew for sure who he was.

Pick Ax.

If I live to be a hundred and five and never see another man as ugly as Pick Ax, I'll die a happy man!! He had a broken nose, buck teeth, flop ears, and one eye that sort of shot out in one direction while the other one looked square at you!! He was as tall, gaunt, and skinny as that Ichabod Crane fella Washington Irving had written about in the *Legend of Sleepy Hollow,* and by God, if they ever declared each day of the year Halloween, well, this fella wouldn't *ever* need a costume, not one single day!! The thing about Pick Ax was that he was a different kind of ugly, not like plug uglies like my old enemies Kragg or Ab Sharpson, but sort of funny ugly, if you know what I mean. The man could give you a laugh at his own expense and still find humor in it without feeling bad, and if you think about it, well, hoss, that shows some sort of character right there.

"Look, Grant," Tom was saying to the depot manager, "the man brought through the valuables and the passengers all in one piece. You can't ask for more than that. Why not give him a chance?"

"Hell, no!" the manager exploded, a gob of tobacco juice mixed in with the spittle that flew from his mouth. "He got my driver killed and that's bad enough. He's fired and stays that way!"

"He's not dead yet, mister," Lisa said in a less than friendly manner. "If I can get this slug out and stop the bleeding, he's gonna pull through."

That manager, well, he had in mind to say something, but you can bet he wasn't about to open his mouth in front of Tom, shotgun or not.

"I'm Tally. You must be Lisa." Tally stepped to the side of the stage driver, across from Lisa, threw back her skirts and said, "How can I help?"

Lisa looked up just long enough to take in Tally's features, then winked at me, a smile on her face. "See, I told you it would be all right." Then, to Tally, "I'd shake hands, but I'm a bit busy right now. Would you hand me one of those pieces of cloth." Tally did as requested and I had the feeling she and Lisa would get along just fine.

"What was in the trunk?" I asked Tally as she worked. "Just clothes?"

"Well, yes, but—"

"Clothes ain't no problem," Tom put in. "We can fit her into some of Lisa's 'til she gets new ones."

"But, what?" I asked.

"She had some books for you, Finn," Sam'l Dean said.

"Books?" I was beginning to feel a deep furrow form across my forehead. Books were hard to come by, and I thought as much of them as Nathan did his collection of Colt revolvers. And if Nathan would fight for that collection, you could be sure I'd go to war over some books, especially if they were ones I hadn't read before.

"One of them was a surprise, Finn," Tally said, looking up for an instant. "I found the third volume in Bancroft's *History of the United States* and brought it with me. I knew you'd like it."

"Don't you worry," I said, the furrows in my forehead growing deeper as a hardness came to my voice. "I will. You can bet on that."

"Uh-oh," I heard Tom say with just a bit of concern.

"He get this way often?" Dean asked Tom with the same amount of caution.

"Only when someone gets uppity with his reading material. He gets worse than a prospector who just struck El Dorado."

"That's what I thought," Dean said. "Last time I seen that look, back in New Orleans, I wound up carrying his deadweight for a longer distance than I care to remember."

"Don't worry, hoss," I said, "you won't be carrying my deadweight this time."

"You mean they's gonna be a fight?" Pick Ax asked, the excitement back in his voice. "Whoopee!"

"Aw, shut up, you old coot," was all Sam'l Dean said.

Chapter 2

"I know it doesn't compare to that house you had in New Orleans," I said, stepping inside our cabin, "but we call it home and it's built better than most."

"After seeing some of those tents and lean-tos on the way up here, I should say so," Tally said, taking in the place.

Those who had decided to make this area their home had put up houses and cabins made of wood and log, taking to the high ground when they did so and for good reason. No one cared to build a house more than once, unless it was a new one for a neighbor or friend, which were usually one and the same. But there were a lot of folks who did just that after last winter's flood of Sacramento. The river had overflowed due to heavy rains, and it was said that near four-fifths of the town was under water at one time. It took a lot of doing to rebuild and restructure what had been damaged, but the one good thing about such disasters is that you get to meet some good people, as Tom and I had done, using our wagons to help people relocate their homes and businesses until everything was right again. Sort of makes a body appreciate what he does have. And that I did.

The cabin was log and bigger than most, and I do believe that if it hadn't been for the help of some of those folks back in Sacramento, Tom and I never would have got it done. Most cabins for a man and wife were measured at fifteen by twenty feet, but this one topped out at forty by sixty. We did it that way to allow room for both Tom and Lisa and Tally and me, with a bit left over for supplies and such. We had found a goodly share of nut pine logs, most of them over a foot in width. Glass was scarce, so the windows were simple wooden shutters that could be opened and closed at will and locked shut when the need arose. Fact is, near everything in the cabin was fashioned of wood, including the beds and cupboards that a cabinet maker had put together for us. Everything except the kitchen stove, the fireplace, and the varied assortment of rifles, shotguns, and pistols that hung from the walls. Most of the rifles and the shotguns were Colt repeaters, the pistols numbering three, each one a different Colt model that held a memory for me.

"The hardest part was building the fireplace," I said as Lisa headed for the kitchen area.

"Whew! I'll say!" Pick Ax remarked, running a finger across his brow as though wiping away profusely pouring sweat. It was all aimed at getting Tally's attention and it did, for she laughed at the man and his antics.

"Hoss, you didn't load none of that stone to bring up here," Tom said.

"Mebbe," Pick Ax replied, "but I druv the wagon to get it up here from the valley!" Then, with a fervent glance at Tally, he added, "Why, ma'am, I used up my whole vocabulary twice over getting them mules up here."

Again Tally laughed, and I knew that as ugly as the man was, she was enjoying his presence. That was one thing about Tally, she was always looking past the outside of a person and trying to find out what went on inside them, and for that I couldn't fault her.

The only reason Pick Ax was with us at the cabin was that Tom, still unable to persuade the depot manager in Sacramento to keep him as a messenger or guard, had agreed to hire him on to ride shotgun for our outfit, considering the trouble we'd run into the day before. At first I had objected, not sure that we could afford to pay another man to work for us. But Tom said that Pick Ax was willing to work for nothing if we agreed to let him eat with us when the women cooked. Which only goes to show what some men would do to be in the presence of a woman, not to mention eat a home-cooked meal. Women were that scarce.

Pick Ax kept his antics up during the meal, giving the women something to laugh at while Tom and I discussed the haul that we were scheduled to make the next day. Since Pick Ax had joined us, I figured that he could ride with Tom while I took the ladies to town to get Tally outfitted. But it was Tally's interest in Lisa and her doctoring abilities that drew our attention back to her.

"You knew exactly what to do when the stage arrived," Tally said, addressing Lisa. "I heard you giving orders even before I was out of the coach. And you knew just what to do once the man was inside. You're quite good, Lisa."

"You better believe it," Tom said with conviction and a hell of a lot of pride. But then, he had always been proud of his wife. Then he took to telling Lisa's story, how she had stowed away with my Ma, Pa, and brother Nathan back in '46 when they were heading west. Tom Dobie had been driving stage at the time and between him and Pa and Nathan and his boy, James, well, Lisa nearly took turns getting saved by each of them from a bounty hunter named Kragg. It was Nathan and I that put a quick halt to Kragg's way of living, but that's a whole 'nother canyon. Ma was with child at the time, and Lisa stuck with us and proved her worth that Christmas morning in '46 when she helped Ma give birth to a new brother for Nathan and me. Ma named him Sean Donovan, taking that middle name from a giant of a man by the name of Alexander William Doniphan. You see, Nathan and Doniphan and I and his outfit were fighting the Mexes at El Brazito and . . . well, like I said, that's a whole 'nother canyon.

"After that Mexican War the Callahans and Lisa and I set down for a while at the base of those Rocky Mountains," Tom said, continuing the story. "Nathan and the rest are still there.

"It was a year later that we got wind of some school back east in Boston, the Boston Female Medical School or something like that, and sent Lisa back to it."

"That explains your proficiency," Tally said. I had the feeling she was pretty impressed with what Lisa'd done.

"It was the first medical school for women," Lisa said proudly, "and I made it in time for the second class."

"I suppose you've met with some problems, even with a medical degree. You know, there aren't too many women doctors in this nation, much less this country, yet," Tally commented.

"At first I did," Lisa said, wrinkling her nose shyly, "but the problems were mostly with the older folks set in their ways. Those fellas down in the valley are so concerned with getting their gold out of the ground that they don't really care who it is that patches 'em up. Besides," she added, throwing a sideward glance at Pick Ax, "I think some of them go out of their way to get hurt just so they can see a woman."

Tally laughed as Pick Ax looked about as embarrassed as I'd ever seen him. Somehow the man's presence seemed to bring an infectious laughter to those around him, and soon we were all having a good laugh, even Sam'l Dean.

The sun was just going down when Tally brought me a last cup of coffee. There was a slight breeze coming up, and being on the high ground like we were, a body tends to notice it more than down in the valley. I was standing off in a small wooded area where I went when I wanted solitude at times. But solitude wasn't what was on my mind just then, and when Tally joined me I felt a warmness that the coffee could never account for. In the background I could hear Pick Ax and Sam'l Dean arguing about something.

"It sounds like they'll be throwing punches at one another any minute," Tally said with a smile, handing me the coffee.

"Not a chance," I said. "You get as old as those two, and complaining about someone is about the only way you've got of saying you like a person. Most of them geezers have been through too much to admit to having a soft spot in 'em."

"I hope we never get that way." She said it in that soft deep-throated voice I had first come to know in New Orleans four years ago. She had a fancy dress on the first time I saw her, and I was dressed in a greasy pair of buckskins, having just come in off a hell-for-leather ride from General Taylor's Army of the Rio Grande, delivering information for some nervous newspaperman I'd met down at Palo Alto. But seeing her that first time, I knew she was the woman I'd fall in love with. And I'll tell you, friend, if it's possible to fall in love in two weeks and actually tell a woman that you want her for a wife at the end of it, well, I reckon I did just that.

I was on my way to Saint Louis to meet Nathan and his wife Ellie and their son James, but I had a couple of weeks to spare and spent them with Tally and Sam'l Dean. Dean had proved out to be her half-brother, and when I left he promised to take care of her. And looking down into her black eyes and that beautiful face, I knew that he had done just that. Or maybe I was just wanting her so much that all I could see was the Tally I'd met so long ago. But I doubted it, for she still had the raven black hair and a way of being strong when she had to be and soft when she wanted to. I don't know if she could see the want in my eyes, but I could sure see it in hers.

"No," I said, taking her in my arms, "I hope we don't ever get that way, either."

We held each other for a while, saying nothing, almost as if we were getting used to one another all over again. It was the first time that day that we'd had any privacy, any chance to be alone together. And believe me, hoss, when moments like that came along, well, you took them when you could, for they were few and far between. In those days it was unlikely that you'd even see a husband and wife kissing one another in public, for that was a private thing and none of anyone else's business. Fact is, I'd seen fathers who'd caught their daughters a-kissing some young lad they'd taken an interest in, and if the old man didn't have his hand on the shotgun when he saw those youngsters, he surely did the next time he laid eyes on the young man. Yessiree, there was a lot of marriages consummated over an innocent kiss. That was why the fella had let out a whistle when he saw

Tally and me kissing at the stage depot. The thing was, neither Tally nor I was too awful innocent about how we felt
about one another, not after those two weeks in New Orleans.

"I missed you," she said after a while, her head buried in
my chest as she held me tight.

"Not half as much as I missed you," I said and slowly
tilted her face to mine and kissed her. We knew that what
each of us had said was true, and maybe that was what made
that kiss linger as long as it did. Whatever the reason, it sure
could stir a man up, that much I'll swear to.

We talked some after that, small talk I reckon you'd call
it, catching up on the past. And other than the run-ins I'd
had with a banker named Esquire back in New Orleans,
every memory I had of my time with Tally was worth
reminiscing over. And I don't think either one of us noticed
the cold in the night air just then.

The next day was going to be a busy one, so I retired early
that night. At least, that was what I had in mind. I remembered the fancy beds that Tally's house had and the citified
way of life that she must have gotten used to as I undressed
that night, wondering what in the hell I could ever offer her
in a wilderness such as this. But she must have had her own
ideas about that, for even with a bed made of only blankets
and buffalo skins, well, Tally had a way of making me feel
right welcome to her.

And to tell the truth, I didn't notice the cold in the air the
rest of that night either.

Chapter 3

The next morning I kept getting strange glances from Tom, the kind that were accompanied with a roguish kind of smile that tells you a man is up to something and that, likely, it's at your expense. If anyone else was in on the joke, they did a fine job of hiding it, for Pick Ax and Sam'l Dean and the women all looked about as perplexed as I was.

"Something bothering you, Tom?" I asked about halfway through our meal. I had that eerie feeling he knew something I didn't, and that can unsettle you right quick.

"No," he said, still smiling, "nothing. It's just that I was remembering something Nathan said before we left his place to come out here."

"Oh?" When he mentioned my brother, Nathan, I started getting real cautious. You had to be around Nathan to know what I mean. I don't think I've ever seen a body as dead serious as Nathan when we had our backs to the wall and the chips were down. But I'll tell you, hoss, when things weren't that way, well, my brother could pull some of the worst practical jokes you've ever seen. I reckon it was his own way of appreciating life, especially after being through some of the scrapes that he and I had. I hadn't seen Nathan for a couple of years now, but all of a sudden I was beginning to know how some of those Indian tribes felt about ghosts and spirits. "And what was that?" I asked.

"Well . . . uh," Tom said finishing his coffee and standing. He was making ready to escape, that much was evident. "Nathan said that once you got your lady friend out here I ought to wait 'til the next morning and then ask you did you test out the wagon springs." His grin broadened about the same time I felt the blood rushing to my face, and I knew Nathan had told him what it meant. I was about to get up and take after him when he set his cup down. "Oh, don't bother showing me the way out." Then, to Tally whose face was also beginning to show some color, he added, "I think your future husband could use another slosh of coffee, Miss Tally."

"Go to hell, Dobie," I said, noticing that the two old men were now having a good laugh over the whole incident, even if they didn't understand it.

"Not today," Tom said from the doorway. "Gotta make a run from the valley. Come on, Pick Ax, we're burning daylight."

"I do believe I'll get the wagon ready for the ladies," I heard Sam'l Dean say, sobering up quicklike. I don't know if it was seeing me mad before that warned him not to push the issue this time or if he figured I was about to explode any minute—which I was—but he made a hasty exit. That left only the women to contend with, and both of them had puzzled looks about them, although I had a notion that Tally knew a little of what was going on.

"Now, what was that all about?" Lisa asked as she and Tally began clearing the table.

I avoided answering just then, telling them I'd wait for them outside. And I did. But the whole time I had only one thing on my mind, and that was breaking Nathan's jaw the next time I saw him!

Sam'l Dean said he'd stay behind and mind the place while we were gone, but just so he didn't get too comfortable I made a point of showing him some deadwood that could have used a good cutting. Some of those old-timers ain't too keen on taking hints, so I said that if he wanted an invite to the shindig that was planned for that night, he had better have us a cord or two of wood stacked high by the time we returned.

"What shindig is that?" Tally asked as she and Lisa got on the buckboard. It was bad enough that Tom and I had to sit on those hard board seats making our freight hauls; in fact when I had the chance I took my horse where I had to go. So I was sorry the women had to ride up there with the splinters.

"You have quite a man here, Tally," Lisa said. Tom's wife hadn't changed much from the first time I'd seen her; she still had a smile and a good choice of words for whoever she happened to see, and with the rotten luck that a good many of the so-called miners had out here, that was exceptional. "All he's been doing since he got your letter saying you'd made the arrangements to come out here is brag to those fellas down in the valley about how pretty a lady he had coming to stay."

The blush that came to Tally's face was one of hidden embarrassment, yet I knew that at the same time she was pleased by the compliment.

"That's a fact," I said. "I got those fellas so worked up about how pretty you are that they said as soon as you got here they wanted to throw a party for you. I reckon Tom'll mention it to 'em when he takes in his load this morning."

"Well, I feel honored," Tally said in her best New Orleans accent.

"You can get rid of that out here, Tally," I said. "You might have to use that voice to impress some of those rich people back there, but out here just being yourself is all that matters." My words must have struck her as out of form, for the look on her face had the same puzzlement as I'd seen earlier. "Honey," I went on, "if you want to impress someone out here, you pick up the nearest piece of wood and hit 'em betwixt the eyes. Works fine on jackasses."

The two women laughed and we headed for Sacramento. I kept to myself for a good share of the trip, while the women palavered about fashions and such woman talk, catching up on what women were wearing in New Orleans and what Lisa had seen in San Francisco since she'd been out here. Tally mentioned that she had packed a few copies of *Godey's Lady's Book,* and it set me to thinking about that trunk of hers that had been stolen. Why would someone steal just that when there was a strongbox in full sight, right where it was supposed to be on the stagecoach? Granted it didn't have anything but a small payroll in it, but that sure was a hell of a lot more than a trunk full of dresses and a few books. It almost seemed as if the trunk had been taken deliberately. Still, Pick Ax might have been right, maybe the outlaws had mistaken the bigger trunk for the cache of gold they were expecting to find. I laughed to myself, thinking of the look that must have been on the faces of those highwaymen when they found out what it was they had stolen. In a way it seemed to justify their taking the wrong box; but I wasn't about to let it go that easily. A man had nearly been killed in that holdup and I was out a couple of books that I had been trying to find for some years now.

Oh, dying was a natural enough thing these days, what with men robbing one another when the gold fever got to be too much for them. It was hard to accept the success of a partner on the claim next to your own when you couldn't scratch out the price of a drink all day long. There were enough stories of bandits and killings over as little as an ounce of gold dust, and thinking on it, I'd have to admit that sixteen dollars an ounce sure did seem like a small price to pay for something worth as much as your life. And I wasn't any too keen on the thought of Tom or me or Pick Ax or any of the rest of us who hauled dust out of the camps to Sacramento and the bigger towns getting shot out of the saddle by some highwaymen who were too damned lazy to make a living for their own selves honestly rather than taking from those who had already done the hardest work getting the gold. No, sirree.

When it came right down to it, at least as far as I was concerned, it went back to what Mr. Jefferson said. From what I'd read about Tom Jefferson, well, it wasn't being the President or writing the Declaration of Independence that the man really wanted to be remembered for in life. It was for founding the University of Virginia. He donated a good share of his books to start that library and the Library of Congress, as I recall, and that was all part of his story, it

surely was. But I reckon what I will always remember about
Mr. Jefferson is what he said about books. "I cannot live
without books," he said, and I reckon I feel the same way.
And, by God, when somebody took to stealing what was
mine—or was about to be mine—well, it didn't do much for
my disposition. Not hardly.

"Finn, are you all right?"

I looked down at Lisa, then Tally, and tried to remember
that I ought to be feeling happy instead of mad.

"You just had the ugliest scowl I've ever seen on your
face," Lisa said with concern. "Are you sure you're all
right?"

I glanced at Tally and winked at her and smiled.

"You bet."

I reckon Tally had some of my sister-in-law Ellie's qualities, if that's what you'd call them. Ellie always seemed to
know when to ask Nathan about something that might be an
unpleasant subject and when to leave him to himself.
There's times a man needs to be by his lonesome, and I
reckon a good woman'll recognize that in her man and let
him be when he needs it. And like I say, it seemed that Tally
was learning right quick about when to ask me what she was
wanting, for it was when she smiled back at me that I felt
good about being there again and put the stagecoach holdup
out of my mind. Hell, it even seemed sort of comical when
she asked me about Tom's remark about the wagon springs
that morning. And if she kept looking at me that way, why I
might not even break Nathan's jaw when I saw him next.
Maybe I'd just twist his arm some.

"When I first went west," I said as we neared the final
stretch before Sacramento, "I took off with an old fella I'd
known most of my life. His name was Cooper Hansen and
we were trailing after Nathan, who'd headed down to Texas
to see a friend of his." Then I went on to explain the whole
business about how I was only fourteen and trying to prove
myself a man and how we'd all of us wound up at San
Jacinto with Sam Houston and his army that April morning
in '36. I never had done much talking about it, but right
then, going back over it and all, I felt a hollow spot in my

belly when I remembered old Cooper Hansen dying that day. It had been one of the bloodiest days of my life and one I'd not soon forget . . . if ever.

"But what does that have to do with the wagon and the springs?" Tally asked. And it's a good thing she did, for I didn't want to dwell on Cooper Hansen and that day.

"Well, Tally," I said, thinking back on it, "by the time me and Cooper Hansen caught up with Nathan, he had already been shot up some and saved by Ellie and her pa, Lije Harper. Fact is, Cooper and I joined in and shot some Comancheros out of the saddle.

"I didn't know it at the time, but Nathan had taken a liking to Ellie. I never noticed it, but I reckon old Cooper had. And that first night Lije, Cooper, and I laid out our bedrolls next to the fire about sunset while Ellie crawled into the wagon where Nathan was sleeping. I came back from tending the horses and asked Cooper what the noise I heard in the wagon was, and he told me it was Nathan and Ellie testing out the wagon springs."

The two women were laughing now, finally aware of what it was that had made Tom Dobie grin so wide and me so mad that morning.

"Oh, but that ain't the joke, ladies," I said as they continued to laugh. When they had calmed down some, I said, "The joke is that the next morning Nathan got asked how the wagon springs was, and I swear I never seen a wounded man more ready to fight in my life." By then I was smiling too, remembering the whole incident as if it were yesterday. Fact was, now that I had it out and told, I might not even twist Nathan's arm next time I saw him. Well, maybe only a little.

"You have quite a family, Finn," Tally said, smiling.

"Oh, that they do," Lisa said, raising an eyebrow, and I knew it wouldn't be long before she was telling Tally her own version of how the Callahans lived. But more important, those two got along fine, which is what I was hoping for. It's bad enough when you've got men competing with each other, but when you throw in two women, well, you're asking for trouble.

It wasn't long before we reached Sacramento, and Lisa took Tally to the general store we had an account at while I headed for the stage depot to see if any more news had come in concerning the outlaws who had bushwacked me and Tom, and the ones who had held up the stage the day before. The manager was still cussing Pick Ax and couldn't give any additional information that would be of use, so I headed for the sheriff's office.

"Nothing new, Mr. Callahan," the sheriff said. "At least, nothing that I've heard of." He was a portly man who looked to be slower than he was. Ray Wallace was pushing forty-five or fifty but was tougher than he looked. I'd seen him take apart a man who outweighed him by a good forty pounds and knew he was capable of holding his own as a lawman. He poured me a cup of coffee and took a seat, inviting me to do the same.

"One thing you could do for me, though, if you've a mind to," he said. "It might help us both out."

"Sure." I shrugged, knowing that what Ray was about to say would be on the level. There were a lot of people who could be bought and sold for any amount of money in that particular area, what with the talk of gold ever on the increase, but Ray Wallace wasn't one of them. He went by the book and took an active interest in the welfare of all who lived in his jurisdiction, whether a prostitute from the red light district or one of the more prominent members of the community.

"Some of the people around here are taking a notion to do like those San Francisco folk and get a vigilance committee formed."

"I can't say as I blame 'em, what with all of the highway robbery that's been taking place."

"It's not just for that, Callahan," he said, a worried look coming to his face. "They mean to do away with the law book and handle *everything* that way. And you know what that means."

That I did. The vigilantes, as they called themselves, had become a self-serving force of justice in the Bay City. Word had come that there had been a number of hangings since they had been formed, and the feeling was that such examples would rid the community of the outlaw element for good. But there had also been stories spread around that some of those who had been hung may not have been guilty of the crimes they were accused of. The trouble was that when a body—or even a group—got that much power and authority to it, well, they didn't seem to care about making a mistake or two. The thought behind it was that if the fella wasn't alive to say anything about it, he wouldn't have any say-so anyway. Yes, I knew what Ray Wallace was talking about.

"What do you want me to do, sheriff?" I asked.

"I hear you're having a bit of a party this evening for that lady friend of yours." I nodded. "Well, if you or your partner gets back this way soon, let me know if those boys out there are talking up this vigilante business. If they are, I'm gonna have to do some talking of my own."

"Don't blame you," I said and assured him that either Tom or I would let him know what we heard, if anything, on the line of vigilante talk.

I left the sheriff's office and was heading toward the general store when I thought I saw Johnstone, the Adams Express man who had made an offer for our line, walking down an alley next to the store. I hadn't liked the man when I first met him and still didn't think favorably of him. He was just too conniving a person to be taken for anything else. I ground-tied my mount and then I saw the women standing by the buckboard waiting for me.

"Find everything you need?" I asked, stepping up on the boardwalk. It was a wasted question, for the back of the buckboard was filled with boxes and packages.

"Most things," Tally said, obviously pleased with what she had bought.

I was about to ask just what "most things" included when another woman came out from around the corner. She was a beauty, I'll say that for her. She had blond hair and a pretty face and a smile that said she knew me from somewhere. But I wasn't prepared for what happened next.

"There you are, darling," she said with a smile and

walked right up to me and kissed me as hard as Tally had the day before when she got off the stage! And if she knew Lisa and Tally were standing there, she sure didn't show it. I wasn't sure what was going on, only that I could feel a warmness in me while she was kissing me. When she backed off, she was still smiling. It was that pleasurable kind of smile that I'd seen on Tally's face after we'd kissed. For one brief second there was silence as she stared at me with that sweet smile on her face, then said, "See you later, sugar," and was gone.

And watching her go was Tally and Lisa, and I do believe I could have counted all their teeth, their mouths were open that wide!

Chapter 4

"And who was that!" Lisa was the first one to speak, after she had gained back her composure. Tally still looked to be in a state of shock over what had happened, and I knew what I saw in those eyes of hers was a fire that would soon be competing with whatever the devil was stoking down in Hades!

"I . . . I don't know." It was all I could think to say, not realizing until then that I was in a bit of shock my own self.

"Then what are you watching her go for?" Those were Tally's first words, and they held a force to them that I hadn't heard for some time.

"Well, I—" I think that all three of us were turning about the color of one of those redwoods, and all for different reasons. "I don't know her, but . . ." And that was the truth. I'd never seen her before.

"She sure knew you," Lisa said, still puzzled as to what was going on. Me, I knew damn well what it was! I was about to experience the way Nathan must have felt the few times I had seen Ellie get mad at him, for there was a vein on the side of Tally's neck that I thought sure would burst any second as she grew redder and redder in the face and madder and madder. Finally, she went to the buckboard, mounting the seat and taking the reins in her hand, all the time giving me a look that could kill.

"Probably some girl on the line," she said with the most

hatred I had ever seen in her. "Come on, Lisa, let's go."
She said it not as a request but as a command and Lisa
obeyed.

I watched them drive off, never looking back at me, and
felt the pain in me like a knife that was being twisted in my
gut. If Tally had meant to hurt me then, that she had. "Girls
on the line" was the term that had come to be known in the
mining camps for the camp followers and prostitutes who
serviced those wanting them. It was common knowledge
that they existed, and although not of the highest moral
code, they were still accepted as part of the way of life on
the frontier. Perhaps they were more civilized about it back
east, but it was still the same cut of cloth. And that was what
hurt the most, Tally's reference to those girls on the line.

I had fallen in love with her the first time I had seen her,
back in New Orleans in '46. She had a mysterious past from
what I was able to find out, but I never was one to judge
other people by what they did way back when. You'd not
find many others who did out here, either. It was the way of
things. But the past Tally had . . . well, she told me about it
not long before I left her. It was one of those ugly stories
about a young girl who had been pushed into the wrong side
of life and found her independence when it was almost too
late. I think I was the only one she ever told, but the ugly
truth was that Tally had started out in life as a prostitute. It
didn't matter to me what she had been; it only mattered that I
loved her and she felt the same about me. But now, with that
wicked look she'd had and the implication that I had taken
up with one of the girls on the line, well, she couldn't have
hurt me worse if she had shot me.

Now, friend, I don't know about you, but there are times
when things get out of sorts in a man's life and he gets to
feeling meaner than a she-bear that's been intruded upon by
someone hunting her cubs. I've seen them get downright
mean and take on whatever or whoever is bothering them,
no matter what their size. And that was how I was feeling
right then.

That Johnstone character had showed up again. I saw him
out of the corner of my eye as I was watching the women

leave in the buckboard and I wouldn't swear that my vision was all that good out of the side of my eyes, what with all the reading I do, but, hoss, I'll tell you, it sure did look like he was coming out of the same alleyway that girl had appeared from. I faced him full and the griz came out of me. Maybe it was coincidence and I should have asked questions first; under any other circumstances I would have, for I'm a peace loving man. But this fella's grin was even broader than Tom Dobie's had been that morning, and he seemed to be having an almighty good time at my expense. Mind you he was bigger than me, but like I said, the griz sort of came out of me then. I was walking toward him of a sudden, and if he noticed the mad on my face, he didn't seem to care, for he just kept on a-smiling.

"You look like you're having woman troubles, Mr. Callahan," was all he said, and that just tore it.

I drove my right fist into his nose, knowing it would take the bite out of him for a second or two, and that was all I needed. I hit him hard three times, all in the face, a right, a left, and a right again before he fell. It didn't knock him out, but if his jaw was feeling anything like my knuckles, he wasn't going to want to do much but back off . . . if he was smart. But I didn't get the chance to find out, for Ray Wallace came walking up at a fast pace, asking what was going on.

"Nothing," I said, glaring down at the big man rubbing his jaw. "This pilgrim just reminded me of my brother, and I took a swing at him." I must have had them confused by that, because both the sheriff and the express agent looked at me as if I were mad. Without another word I got on my horse and headed out of town, rubbing my knuckles.

To hell with hitting Nathan! When I saw him next, I'd just shake his hand and tell him the story.

"Yep," Sam'l Dean said, sadly shaking his head as I got off my horse, "he's in trouble again. I shouldda knowed it."

He was stacking wood next to the cabin as he spoke to Tom and Pick Ax. Just as sure as a frown appeared on

Dean's face when he said it, Pick Ax seemed to light up like a Roman candle. "And don't you say a thing!" Dean added, pointing a warning finger at his counterpart. Pick Ax, at his comical best, showed a hurt, resentful look and he walked away in a huff.

"Been trying to knock them sequoias with your bare fists again, have you?" Tom said, half in jest, as I rubbed my knuckles.

"Might as well have been," I said and told Tom of what happened as I fished out some liniment to fix myself up.

I'd been riding most of the afternoon, just by my lonesome, out away from any kind of civilization. I had no regrets about what I'd done to Johnstone, none at all, but I wouldn't have been any good around people the way I was feeling. So getting away from everyone seemed to be the best thing to do at the time. Usually I could go riding and take in the country and what Mother Nature had seen fit to put on the land, and it would be enough to convince me that no matter what happened I still had all of this beautiful country. But that afternoon all I could think of was how I might be losing Tally and how the country wouldn't be worth anything unless I could live in it here with her by my side.

"Lisa told me what happened," Tom said when I had finished.

"Are they here?" I found myself asking a bit too quickly. The thought was in the back of my mind that if I could see Tally and explain to her again, make her understand, that things would be right again.

"No. The girls left early," Tom said, pausing, then he glanced at me with a raised eyebrow. "Went down into the valley to do some cooking for that shindig tonight. Or so they said. Seems old Flaherty's wife is gonna let 'em use some of her dutch ovens to do some baking in."

"Oh." I must have sounded as let down as I felt and I turned to go to the cabin.

"Finn."

"Yeah, Tom," I said over my shoulder.

"Don't be too hard on her. She's likely just . . . excited about being in a new land. You know how women are, it takes 'em time to get settled in. Shoot, old Pick Ax and Dean could live anyplace out here, including one of them mountain tops, they been here that long.'' He chuckled. "Hell, they probably helped Moses carry the Commandments down from the Mount and claimed it was Pike's Peak. And you and me been out here long enough to make our way. It's expected. But women, that's a whole different breed of she-lion.''

"I don't know if I'm ready for any more of what happened today, Tom,'' I said and again started to leave.

"Finn.''

"Yeah.''

"Don't be too hard on your own self, pard.'' When I squinted at him, he added, "This ain't no one-horse operation, 'cause your saddle's throwed into it too. If she don't need you, hoss, I do. We still got ore to haul.''

"Sure.''

Tom had changed some since I'd first met him in Saint Louis back in '46, driving the stagecoach that brought my family and Lisa west. Tom was gruff and as hard-talking then as any driver ever had been or would need to be. He talked more to his animals than he did to the humans he hauled in his coach, and said one time he preferred horses to most people because they, at least, did what they were told.

Eighteen forty-six had turned out to be a hard year for a lot of folks, most of them being Mexicans who went up against a passel of us volunteers who were just itching for a fight. Ironically, we wound up in Mexico at a place called Sacramento down there fighting the Mexicans against four-to-one odds. I don't believe I've ever seen a bunch of rag-tag men that looked as misfit to fight as we did. And I reckon the Mexes thought the same, but it was a big mistake on their part. I found out a long time ago that just cause there ain't no flame don't mean you can't get burnt by the embers; and hoss, that's *just* what we taught those Mexicans that day.

But it was before that battle that I found out Tom Dobie planned on doing some changing from that hard-crusted driver I had first met. Oh, he fought as hard as the rest of us that day, but just before we marched into what seemed like certain death, I heard him and Lisa telling each other how much they loved one another. And that does things to a man. I know, because I felt the same way about Tally. Or at least I thought so. There's something inside you that makes you fight harder to stay alive and protect your woman no matter what. Maybe it's because this is a big land and a body can get awful lonesome out here if he ain't careful. And having someone like Lisa or Ellie . . . or Tally . . . well, I reckon it makes whatever hardships you're going through worth it.

Remembering that gave me a new determination to set things straight with Tally. I'd do it tonight at the shindig; get myself cleaned up and put on some new clothes. Yes, I'd give it another try. Hell, Tally was worth it!

"Whatcha smiling at?" Tom asked.

"Oh, nothing," I said, having no intention of telling him what I had on my mind about me and Tally. "It's just that I've never heard you philosophize about women that way before."

"Phil who?" A look of puzzlement came to his face. "Finn, I told you before, I don't know none of those fancy fellas with ten dollar names. I was just speaking my mind."

"Sure, Tom," I said, still smiling, "just speaking your mind."

One thing I had found out about mining camps was that when a woman showed up you could depend on civilization setting in in one form or another. Just let them at it and their imaginations would run wild with all sorts of things they remembered from back east. I'd seen some camps that had set up their own community library and others that brought in a padre or minister for services occasionally. The frontier didn't have many churchgoers just then, for many a miner who might have desired attending regular services was just too tired to do it. But one thing you found out right quick was that even if he didn't go to services that often, well, a man working in some of the bigger mines had to have one powerful faith in his Maker to get him through the day. That was for sure!

I never was certain, but I had a suspicion that somehow a woman had been involved in the new style of clothing that was being worn. I knew Nathan would be wearing buckskins until the day he died, simply because it was what he had been introduced to when he became a frontiersman. There was likely something else behind it, probably his stubbornness that kept him from changing. Me, I've always been looking for newness in life and am willing to accept a bit of change now and then. And that was what I found on Tally's bed alongside the opened packages. Oh, she had her some dresses and women's things and such, but right along with them were what looked to be men's denims.

Word had it that a fella by the name of Levi Strauss had sailed from somewhere on the East coast on around the Horn here to California in '49 with supplies of cloth. Upon arrival here he sold all of his stock except for some bales of canvas he had meant to sell to miners to be used in the making of tents. Now, hoss, mining just ain't one of your leisurely rich-man schemes to make a bundle of money. No, sirree. It's usually the fellas who supply the goods for such expeditions that are the ones who get rich overnight. Having to grapple with Mother Nature—and in some cases Father Time—most of your waking hours tend to be hard on what you're wearing. And it doesn't take long to figure out that if you ain't got a good supply of clothes laid in for the duration, why you'll likely spend your second month panning for gold in not much more'n your birthday suit. I reckon that was why those miners figured they needed good, sturdy clothes about then more than they needed tents, and that's what they elected for.

Of course, there was another story going around claiming that this Strauss fella had taken on a bet that he could make clothes that would be strong enough for a western man's needs. If you believed that one, he had won his bet, but like I said, if it had to do with clothing, well, hoss, you can bet that there was a woman collecting on the bets!

That was one other thing I'd been noticing. That Industrial Revolution that Ma and Pa had mentioned so long ago before I left home back in '36 was still going strong in this country. And it seemed like everything that came along had its name—as rightfully it should—from the man more than the invention. Sam Colt had been putting out his firearms for the better part of fourteen years now and Colt's pistols had become as important to anyone west of the Mississippi as a bowie knife. I reckon it just seemed like people were getting a bit more personal about their tags on certain things, for those denims on Tally's bed hadn't become known as Strauss's denims as one might have figured, but rather as *Levi's* denims. I cleaned up and changed into a pair of my own Levi's.

As dangerous as times were, at a shindig like the one I was going to most miners would stack arms just out of politeness if they knew there would be women present. You can bet those arms weren't stacked too far away, but they did it just the same, so I figured I'd leave my Dragoon and the holster I'd fashioned for it at the cabin. Carrying my bowie wouldn't be that out of place, for a body had to have something to cut a slab of meat with. What they wouldn't see was the little surprise I'd be carrying elsewhere.

I rode down to the valley where the men looked more life-size than they did being looked down on from our cabin. Tom and I knew most of them by name, for we hauled their ore for them as often as need be. You get to trusting one another when you're dealing with each other's livelihood, and when it ain't business that you're seeing them about, well, hoss, you get down right neighborly. I rode slow into the camp, nodding here and there or saying a howdy-do to those I knew better than others. But what I was really doing was looking for Tally and Lisa. Ain't no man likes to be wrong, and a man hunting up his woman after the sort of fandango we'd been through, well, it was a belittling thing to be doing, so I tried to look as casual as I could.

"Just like a woman," I said when I rode up to the two of them setting up any variety of dutch ovens with Flaherty's wife. "Trying to do everything by your lonesome. Can I give you a hand with those?" I was trying to be as pleasant as a body could and had the feeling Tally was doing the same. She smiled at me briefly and might have spoken had it not been for the Flaherty woman.

"Hmmph!" was all that came out of her as she stuck an indignant nose in the air and took Tally's arm. "Come, Tally, George will help us with these."

I watched her go, or maybe it was Tally I was watching and this woman just got in the way. George Flaherty was one of those small men who, somehow, got hooked up with a woman who tried to be the boss at everything. And I do believe that George was the only one who had a rein on her. The books I had read would call Althea "ample" to be sure, but the truth was she had more chest than George ever would. Fact was, I wondered at times if they were ever going to have any youngsters, for I had a hunch old George might just smother himself to death in that baby making . . . if you know what I mean. But like I say, he had a rein on her and knew how to handle her. He was the kind of man who'd wait for her to get good and mad and then have her sit on his shirt and trousers once he found a flat board so he could get them dried and pressed all at one time. And, hoss, that's ingenuity.

"I could use some help," Lisa said with a smile.

I ground-tied my mount and gave her a hand setting up those ovens and feeding wood to them while she set to making several kinds of batters on one of the community tables. I was slow and deliberate about my task, not wanting to appear as anxious as I was, but Tally didn't return and I found myself wondering if she had fled me again.

"She'll be back, Finn," Lisa said.

"Huh? Oh, yeah."

She paused a moment before speaking again, studying something in my face, I reckon. I never was sure, for I had my mind on other things just then. "You two have got me worried," she said, placing a hand on my arm. "Here I was expecting to plan a big wedding and now this happens."

"Don't go worrying about it, Lisa. I need to talk to her, to explain some things." I winked at her, smiled, although I'm sure it was a weak one. "But don't you worry none, it'll only give you gray hairs. Besides, worrying's like riding one of them rocking horses.'' She frowned at me in a curious sort of way, the kind that said she wasn't following my trail. ''It'll keep you busy,'' I added, ''but you don't get a damn thing done.'' She smiled then, and I looked past her to the layout on the table. ''And it seems to me you got an awful lot to do right now. Why don't you get to it, and I'll see if I can't round up Miss High and Mighty and Tally and have 'em give you a hand.''

''Sure, Finn,'' she said and I knew she was feeling better about things. I also knew the food would taste a hell of a lot better now that she could concentrate on it. I hadn't quite told her the truth just then, but there wasn't any reason the rest of them at this shindig should be any the worse for wear, be it from the cooking or anything else. There were problems in a man's life, his business for example, that he could share with others who would give him a hand if need be. But what was between a man and a woman, well, it wasn't something that you discussed all that much with others, for those affairs were private.

I found Tally not far off with Althea still at her side, likely trying to get more of the sordid details about what had happened.

''Mrs. Flaherty,'' I said, ''Lisa could use some help with whatever it is she's putting together.'' When she didn't budge, I said, ''Now, ma'am.'' I was getting fed up with arrogance being the order of the day, especially with this woman, so I said it hard.

The Flaherty woman was facing me now, a purely indignant look about her, as though she had been insulted. Well, hoss, I had a surprise for her.

''Tally,'' I said, all the time looking straight at Mrs. Flaherty, ''your friend here reminds me of some of them stuffed shirts back in New Orleans. Walking around like a dog peed on their leg, with their nose stuck so far up in the clouds you could swear they were kissing Saint Peter on the . . . feet.''

''Well, I never!!'' The fat woman said it with the righteous indignation of the times that was the hint that a man was supposed to pull in the reins right then and there, for she'd have no more of my backtalk. But like I said, she was in for a surprise.

"You want to watch saying things like that ma'am," I said, my eyes never leaving her. "A body might take to thinking you're something you ain't."

The look that came to her face was like seeing Tally all over again that morning, for she turned a beet red that would have made Tally look pale even then. I knew I'd have to settle with George Flaherty later on for what I'd said, but what had taken place seemed to break the ice for Tally and me. Mrs. Flaherty went steaming off in a huff that could have powered a Mississippi riverboat, and I saw Tally break into a smile as she watched the woman leave.

"Finn, that was terrible," she said still smiling and still, for the moment, at least, her old self again.

"I know," I said, getting over the mad I had felt toward the other woman, "it's one of those traits I picked up from my brother." Then I remembered what I had come for and the beginning of a smile was gone from my face. "But it wasn't half as terrible as what you did to me this morning."

"Yes," she said, the smile now gone from her face, too. "I suppose it isn't." I wasn't but arm's length from her now, and when she avoided my look, I slowly tilted her chin back, forcing her to face me. The look on her face was one of hurt that I hadn't seen in a long time, not since that time in New Orleans. I knew it was paining her, what she'd said that morning, probably as much as it was me, but there was something she had to know and if I didn't say it now I knew I never would.

"Tally, I love you," I said. "You've got to believe it. I always have and always will. I never saw that woman on the street before in my life. The only reason I can think of her doing what she did was to make you jealous, and it seems that she succeeded.

"I don't know why you lashed out the way you did, Tally, but you'd better know that this ain't no big-time society out here where you can potshot people one day and call them friends the next. When you cut to the bone out here, it's not something to be done lightly, for it isn't taken lightly. It's a hard life and you take the nice things as they come because they are few and far between. And when you spoil 'em, it's like bad meat; you can't do nothing but get rid of it and move on." I had both hands on her shoulders now, squeezed them gently. "And, Tally, I don't want to move on. I want to stay right here with you.

"Look, Tally, do you remember me telling you about my brother, Nathan? About his obsession with Sam Colt's pistols?" She nodded silently. "Well, he puts every bit of trust in those guns to bring him through when he gets between a rock and a hard place. And he's right, for a man's got to put his trust in the things and people he knows are gonna carry him through in this land." For a man who did a lot of reading I was finding the right words hard to come by. "It's the same way with me and Tom. We partnered with each other 'cause we know each can trust the other." My voice softened and I looked her straight in the eye as I spoke, for I wanted her to know it was the truth I was speaking. "Maybe most important of all, Tally, is that you've got to have that same kind of trust between a man and a woman out here, or else . . . or else it just ain't gonna be."

I was expecting her to say something by way of explanation, but all she did was rush into my arms and hold on like she never wanted to let loose again, and I reckon that was all that needed be said. We held each other in silence for a while.

"I don't want to live without you, Finn," she finally said, still holding me. "It's just that some things bring up . . . old habits that are . . . hard to break." It was said in a halting manner, the way you say something that you know you've got to get out but ain't too proud of saying all the same. And I had a hunch I knew what she meant by those "old habits" she mentioned, and as far as I was concerned, they weren't worth talking about.

"I understand."

She looked up at me, smiled, and gave me another hug, running her hands up and down my back as she did, stopping dead stock still when she reached the small of my back.

"What on earth is that?" she asked, running her hand slowly over the bulge under my jacket.

I reached behind me and pulled out the Colt's. She had seen me with my Walker-Patersons down in New Orleans in '46, and I had watched her look in awe at the Walker Colt that hung in my room. But this one was a different type and it, too, held her fascination.

"It's a smaller version of the pistol I carry," I said, hefting it in my hand. "A pocket pistol, most call it. I call it my little surprise. I was gonna give it to you and show you how to use it."

"Really?" She carefully took the pistol from my hand, closely examining it. It was the first time I'd seen a woman take that much of an interest in a six-gun before, and for a minute it sort of threw me. Hell, the way she was looking over that Colt's, she sure wasn't acting like she needed any familiarization with it.

"It's so . . . plain," she said, handing it back to me.

"Yeah, but it get's the job done and that's what counts out here." And that was the God's honest truth!

The pistol she had been looking over was one of the first pocket pistols that Sam Colt had put out in 1848. You might call it the baby sister of the Dragoon revolver he put out at the same time, and the truth of the matter was that the smaller one was selling just a bit faster than that bigger one.

One thing you found out right quick when you ventured past the Mississippi; if there was anything to be had in the way of firearms, most frontiersmen would take the bigger one over the smaller, and with good reason. Unless you intended on eating squirrel and prairie chicken the rest of your born days, you'd have to have something bigger than some of those peashooters I'd seen some of those city folk carrying back in New Orleans. Pepperboxes and derringers were fine for arguing over cards, but a body would starve to death on the plains if he tried to bag his supper that way. So I reckon Sam Colt was doing his best to please both the city folks and us plainsmen.

The original Dragoon was nothing more than a scaled

down version of the Walker Colt that put Sam back in business during the Mexican War. Don't get me wrong now, that Walker was one hellacious weapon, both to fire and be looking down the business end of! But it was just too damned heavy for a man to carry other than on his horse. So what Sam did was trim off some of the weight and temper the load on the Walker and the result was the First Model Dragoon. It had the same features of the Walker, including the squared-back trigger guard. The barrel was seven and a half inches, and it still fired a .44 slug but with less of a load than the Walker had. And, most important to a lot of us, it weighed in at just a tad over four pounds which took about a pound off the Walker's weight when it was fully loaded. One pound difference may not seem like much to someone who doesn't know about guns, but to a man on the frontier it made *all* the difference. Besides, I sat down one time and thought on it, and I reckon the reason that most men didn't favor carrying that Walker on their hip is that it can get kind of embarrassing trying to explain to your lady friend how you come by getting calluses on your hip bones . . . if you know what I mean.

But it was the Dragoon's baby sister, the Baby Dragoon that some were calling it now, that had outsold the big .44. I never did figure out why, maybe there's just more gamblers and city folk than there are us types on the frontier, a fact which was getting to be harder to believe each day as more prospectors came to the camps of California looking for a lifetime's worth of gold in just a few days or weeks.

The Baby Dragoon—the one I was giving Tally—came in a .31 caliber with a four-inch barrel, although you could get them in damn near any size from three to six inches in length. Scaled down like it was, it only weighed a couple of pounds and could be easily concealed in a man's coat pocket or one of the oversized pockets on a woman's dress. Or stuck in the small of your back as I had made a practice of doing. The design was similar to the Paterson that Sam Colt had put out, for the weapon was a five-shot and had no loading lever, as did the bigger .44. What Sam had done was require the carrying of a second loaded cylinder, or if you had your own powder and ball and caps, you could use the axis pin which had a cupped end to it to reload with. Thinking like that was just short of being a genius to a man on the frontier, and you can bet there were a lot of us that let Sam Colt know so.

"What's so funny?" I asked when she started to giggle.

"It's ironic," Tally said, still confusing me with that mischievous giggle of hers. I'm not as scared of women as my brother Nathan is, but I never did get used to not being let in on the secret when someone started acting like Tally was now, or Tom had this morning. It was just unsettling.

"I don't understand."

"Well, Finn, here you are giving me this handgun of yours, and one of the surprises I had for you was one just like it that I had ordered."

"You're joshing me, right?"

"No," she said, still smiling. "After the interest you showed in those pistols of yours, I decided that next to a good book, you'd probably appreciate one of them as a gift. So, when you sent word that you wanted me to come out here, I wrote your Mr. Colt and mentioned that I knew you and that I wanted to make a present of one of his guns to you." Of a sudden her smile was gone and I knew she was remembering the same thing I was, that the trunk she had brought had been stolen. "But, I suppose I'll no longer be able to do that."

"It doesn't matter," I said, "as long as you're here." I kissed her then, and she quickly ran away like some school girl who had just stolen her first kiss. And I don't mind telling you that I enjoyed watching her run like that.

Knowing that she had gone to the trouble to have one of Colt's pistols made for me made me even that much more determined to find that trunk that had been stolen. That particular event was still a puzzle to me. But for that matter, everything that had been happening since just before Tally arrived had been confusing. The attempted holdup of our outfit, the stagecoach robbery, a strange woman kissing me like some long-lost lover, and the Johnstone man wanting to buy us out. Perhaps it was coincidence, but there was too much of it going on at one time to believe that at least one or two of the incidents hadn't been staged for my benefit. The woman was a plant for sure, that much I knew. Someone was wanting to disrupt what Tally and I had, a deep love for each other. And that Johnstone character was in on it, of that I was certain too. He had looked too damned smug after the incident with the woman not to have been involved somehow. But how?

The holdup of the stage that Tally had been on didn't sound anything like the highway robberies that we usually heard about in this area either. Yet, it had happened and everyone else was of the mind that the taking of Tally's trunk full of clothes was a fortunate mistake, at least for whoever's payroll had been in the driver's boot that day. Perhaps I was being overly concerned because the trunk had contained presents that Tally had intended for me, but thinking about it made me mad and I decided to put it out of my mind for the time being. There had been enough misunderstandings for the day without creating any more, and I thoroughly intended to enjoy the party that night.

And that I did.

To no one's surprise, Tally, Lisa, and the Flaherty woman had spent a few hours baking breads, doughnuts, and other such things that a man found scarce in a mining camp. A steer had been put to slaughter and was roasting on an open fire and a good time was being had by all.

"I didn't think any of these miners could stand to kick up their heels after working a full day in the mines," Tally said in disbelief after she'd been invited again to take a twirl around the space that served as our dance floor.

"Bring a woman to a shindig like this," Tom grinned, "and these fellas will find energy they didn't know they had."

All of that dancing must have been wearing her out, for she refused as politely as she could two offers to dance as another tune was struck up. It was surprising the amount of musical talent that had been put together for the party. Several of the men showed up with fiddles and guitars, as well as a few horns of various shapes and sizes. Some of the noises coming from them would never make it to a concert, but those were overlooked and the general sound of them carried the dancers through their movements well enough. I had danced the first few dances with Tally and had shared her with the rest of the miners since.

"Miss Tally, here's some punch," I heard Pick Ax say as he came up behind us. He handed a tin cup to her as she graciously curtsied to him with a smile.

"Why, thank you, Pick Ax."

"Yessum." He seemed a bit uneasy as he glanced back at Mrs. Flaherty standing guard over the punch bowl. "Whew, that woman can be mean."

"Oh?"

"Yessum," he said, a frown on his face. "Said I was so ugly my feet didn't even match."

"She ain't much of a prize her own self," I said, throwing in my two cents' worth.

"You got a point, Finn," Tom said, throwing a glance toward the big woman. "Man married her must've been awful desperate."

"No man could be that desperate," Pick Ax said. "Likely she took him to the altar with a shotgun in his back."

Tally laughed at the comment, and I knew she was enjoying herself as much as I was.

"Mr. Pick Ax, would you do me the honor of being my partner for this next dance?" she said with a smile.

"Who, me?" the old-timer said, looking as though he had been struck by a grizzly bear. "You're asking me?"

"Yes. You are Mr.—"

"Oh, yes, ma'am, that's me all right!"

He sounded as though he was getting the golden opportunity of a lifetime and was afraid it would disappear before his eyes. But it didn't take much to tell that his dream had come true when the fiddles started up again and a proud look came to his eye as he escorted Tally out on the floor, dusty as it was.

Most of the night was like that. We all had a good time, and even Sam'l Dean took Lisa for a dance. To hear him complain as much as he did, you'd swear he couldn't be as spry as he was with a woman on his arm, but it didn't stop him from having a good time.

Neither Tom nor I heard any talk of vigilantes or lynch mobs as Ray Wallace had suspected, and finally, at the end of that day, I had the feeling that all was right with the world.

Chapter 5

"—Damn it!!"

The way Tom was cussing, you'd have thought the whole valley would hear him. Lisa raised an eyebrow as she finished pouring coffee, while Sam'l Dean and Pick Ax frowned at one another. Tally was just plain surprised at being able to hear Dobie way out in the corral while we were finishing breakfast.

"Something's gone wrong?" Tally asked.

"Sounds like it," I said, rising from the table as Lisa took away the coffeepot. "One way or another I'm gonna hear about it, and I reckon now is as good a time as any."

I sloshed on my hat and headed toward the corral where Tom usually hitched up the teams for our runs. For the few years I had known him, he was the best man I'd ever seen with a team of horses, mules, oxen . . . anything! I also knew that when my partner started cussing a blue streak like I was hearing as I approached the corral and tool shed, well, hoss, he didn't often do it for nothing. When I got close enough I could see what had made his blood boil and felt mine go through the same process.

"What in the hell?" I heard myself mutter as I looked from Tom's red face to the harness in his hand.

"Cut!!" he said, trying his best to stay calm. "Clean through."

"I'll say." I set down the cup of coffee I had brought and

fingered the edge of the harness. Most of our equipment had seen a good bit of wear, but Tom and I always kept it in the best of shape, and even the piece in my hand wasn't worn enough to have simply fallen apart. "Pard, whoever did it had a good, sharp knife."

"That's what I figure," Tom said, taking the scalding cup from the fencepost and drinking near all of the liquid. If he burned his mouth, he didn't show it. But then, he was likely too mad even to think about it. He tossed aside the remaining contents and handed me the cup, a stern look on his face. "Get the guns," he said. It was an order, not a request. "I'm getting the horses."

"Sure, but—"

"Just get 'em!" He turned to walk toward the barn as I did the same to the cabin. I'd only taken a few steps when I heard his hard voice again. "And Finn?"

"Yeah," I said over my shoulder.

"Bring along that revolving shotgun your friend, Colt, gave you. We're going after bear and I got a hunch we're gonna need more'n two shots to bag old Ezekiel."

"Ezekiel?" Tally said, standing in the doorway, a curious look on her face.

"That's what he said." I walked on past her and began gathering guns and some extra powder and ball as Tally followed me.

"Ezekiel?" This time she said it with that lilt a woman has to her voice when speaking of something unbelievable.

"It's a term conjured up by the mountain men some time back when they came out here," I said, trying to do two things at one time. "It was what they said when they refered to the Devil, as I recall. And after meeting up with a grizzly bear once in a while they started calling them 'Old Ezekiel' too." I'd had more than one run in my own self with bears and knew good and well why those old mountain men like Nathan's father-in-law Lije Harper called the griz Ezekiel. A body might's well meet up with the Devil himself if he was to get out alive from under the paw of a griz! "Tom, now, he claims to have spent some time with those trappers, so whenever he gets set on something, why he just says 'We're a-going after Old Ezekiel.' "

"Sort of part of the partnership, saying 'we'?" Tally said with a smile.

"Yeah," I said, reaching for the Colt Revolving Shotgun on the wall pegs. "But I got a feeling the bear we're going after ain't got quite as much hair on it as Old Ezekiel."

"Is there going to be a problem?"

There was concern in her voice, so I reassured her that Tom and I were just going to do some talking to a few people. I just didn't tell her that it was going to be to that Johnstone fella in particular. Nor did I mention just how we were going to do our talking. There were times when a man's fists and guns are as good a substitute for talk out here as his words, and I had a feeling Tom and I were going to wind up using more than just the English language to do our talking this time. But a woman ought not to be worried like that, so I told Tally it was going to be all right.

"Where do you think you're going?" I asked Pick Ax as Tom brought the horses to the cabin. The old-timer had that toothless grin about him that spelled mischievousness. He knew when there was trouble a-coming and had it in mind to tag along.

"Why, with you two, 'carse," he said in that drawn-out mountain accent of his. "That's why you got the shotgun, ain't it?"

"Not hardly, old-timer," Tom said. "I want you and Dean here to see what you can do about fixing up those harnesses out by the shed."

"Shoot, boy, you're gonna go off and have all the fun!" He said it as if he were a youngster who hadn't gotten his way.

"Fun, my aching . . . back," Dobie fired back at him, taking a glance at the two women present before finishing the sentence.

"Lisa, didn't you say you were going to show me how to make something called 'bear sign' today?" Tally was dead honest in what she said, but I knew what she was trying as well as the rest. Even Sam'l Dean had a smirk on his face.

"Oh! Oh, yes!!" Lisa said absentmindedly. "I almost forgot."

"Bear sign!" Pick Ax's eyes lit up at the mention of the western term for doughnuts. They could be a rarity, indeed, but then, most anything a woman cooked out here was considered a rarity.

"Sure," Tally said. "Why we ought to have a batch ready by the time you and Sam'l get those harnesses mended."

Pick Ax had a decision to make now as he glanced back and forth between Lisa and Tom Dobie. I reckon the thought of good food and being able to look at a pretty woman while you ate it might well sway any man, for he grudgingly agreed to stay without further argument. But I swear I saw a longing look in his eye as Tom and I left, as though he were telling himself that if it were anything but bear sign, he'd be riding right down the trail beside us.

"Johnstone?" I asked when we started down the trail.

Dobie nodded. "You're thinking along the same lines as I am."

"I thought so. I saw you talking with him some last night at the party. He still trying to buy us out?"

"Yup." Tom was silent a moment as his face began to grow red again, the anger renewed. I'd seen Comanches who could have killed four men after they'd been shot dead that looked friendlier than my partner just now.

"But he's gone too far this time," Tom went on.

"How's that?"

"He said no pack mule express was gonna get out from selling to him. Said one way or another he'd have us, rigs, horses, and all. Now, Finn, I can tolerate some shenanigans . . . Hell, ain't the first time I've ever had my riggings cut to pieces. But I'll tell you, hoss, stuff like this just leads to more serious kinds of foolishness, and I'll be damned if anyone's gonna try something with my horses." With that he spurred his horse and rode ahead.

Me, I trailed behind him, giving him time to work off some of the mad that was in him now. One thing that Johnstone was going to learn was to be awful careful about making Tom mad. Or else he was going to have to make himself awful scarce when he did.

They called us the "pack mule express," "us" being the independents who worked an outfit like Tom and I did, while "they" were the bigger outfits, like the Adams Express Company that Johnstone represented. So far it was one of the biggest in the area, but there was talk of an outfit that was being formed by a couple of fellas named Wells and Fargo that would give it competition. To be sure, our rates were often cheaper than those of the bigger companies, but we were restricted by the amount we could haul. If there wasn't so much highway robbery in the area, as we now knew from personal experience, Tom and I would have run two wagons instead of the one we did. As it was, one of us was needed to drive while the other rode shotgun. Like I said, Tom was the best I'd seen with a team, so he did the driving while I carried the hardware. So far we'd been lucky.

Watching Tom ride ahead of me, I got to wondering just what he had in mind for Johnstone when we got to town. I had no objection to taking the man down a notch or two, not after the smug expression I'd seen on his face yesterday, not at all. But Tom had the look of a man who has the urge to kill, and I knew he could do it when called upon. The problem was that I hadn't gotten used to going around starting trouble. Hell, it was hard enough just keeping out of it without having to stir up your own batch of it. And riding the river with Tom Dobie when trouble started could be a bit like standing next to one of those engineers who set the dynamite charges in the mines. They might know what they were doing, but you damn sure didn't want to be around when fate took a hand and upset the cart!

It was close to noon when we got into town, and in a way I was glad of it, for I pursuaded Tom to get a bite to eat before we went hunting Johnstone. We spent an hour at that meal, getting some mighty strange looks while we did. What I was trying to do was stall Tom for time; what I wound up doing was looking like some kind of fool. I came on the idea remembering the story I'd heard about the Euro-

pean tourist who had been going through the area and had
stopped in one of the bigger cities and better restaurants on
his way. And he happened to be taking his meal at the same
time some grubby-looking frontiersman miner who had just
struck it rich was taking his. Now, friend, we just got too
much to do out here to do much more than eat a meal because it's a necessity; unless, of course, a woman, or two,
does some baking—then it becomes an event! So we eat our
meals and get on with our business most times. But this Eu-
ropean fella, why he took his own sweet time eating every
bite of his meal as easy as you please. So the miner, on leaving, walked over to the foreigner, gave him a strange look,
and said, "Mister, you look like you're trying to *enjoy* that
food!" To which the gentleman calmly replied, "As a matter of fact, I am." It was that strange kind of look I was getting while I tried to keep Tom at the table.

Finally, there was no more excuse to stay, and we headed
over to the saloon where we had first met Johnstone two
days before. A man like him usually had a liking for free
drink and tall stories, so I had no doubt we'd meet him there
again.

We did. Only, it wasn't quite what I expected.

Tom had a temper, but he knew I preferred talking to
going root hog or die and jumping in with both feet before
you found out it's quicksand you're jumping into. We had
been in situations like this before, and I'd managed to keep
Tom from coming to any serious harm and expected to do
the same now. Johnstone was bellied up to the bar, talking
to three others who, by their dress and talk, I assumed to be
associates of his. And I had to admit to myself that I was getting curious as to just what the big man would have to say to
Tom's accusations.

"Mr. Johnstone," I said as we approached him, "we'd
like to talk to you about something."

Johnstone, who'd had a smile on his face while talking to
his friends, turned to me and said, "Oh, you," as the smile
vanished.

That's when Tom hit him. He was carrying the Colt shotgun in his left hand and hit the big man with a beefy hard

right. As Johnstone sailed backward, more out of surprise
than hurt, Tom quickly brought the butt of the shotgun into
the side of the man next to Johnstone. If the man was an innocent bystander, he didn't stay that way as his hand went to
his side and fire came to his eyes. Tom hit the man with a
right cross again and set down the Colt shotgun on the bar as
he went after Johnstone.

I never should have spoken to Johnstone in the first place!
The man who was already mad and two others were coming
at me now as Tom and Johnstone traded blows toe to toe. I
kicked out a chair at one of Johnstone's pals as he tried to
leap for me and he caught his foot on the chair rung and fell
face first to the floor. All I could do now to keep from being
beaten to death was back up, but someone who wanted to
fight gave me a push from the rear and I found myself being
propelled toward the second man as he brought a knee into
my stomach. It must have been the third one, the one who'd
been hit in the side, who drove a fist into me then as I fought
to keep from blacking out. That was when I saw the foot
next to me and stomped on it as hard as I could. It produced
a yell to my right and I swung out at it, hoping I'd catch him
right under his belt buckle.

I did.

Seeing the pain on his face didn't make me feel any better, but you can bet I wasn't feeling sorry for him either. I
swung at him with my left and it's a good thing I did, for I
felt the wind of a missed swing against the back of my ear as
I moved against him. But I didn't stop there, spinning to get
ready for the man I knew was behind me now. I must have
been off balance because when I had completed my turn, the
man who had just missed made sure he wouldn't do it again.
Like Johnstone, he was a big one, and the force of his blow
sent me back into the man I'd just hit, sending both of us
sprawling to the floor. My chest and side were sore, but I
wasn't about to be caught on the floor. I rolled to the side,
trying to get in a crouching position to rush the man, but as I
did I saw him lunge for the Colt shotgun at the bar. At the
same time the whole room erupted into one big valley of

echoes as some kind of cannon went off and I heard the sound of buckshot richocheting against the walls.

The man was at the bar, his hands on the shotgun, but he was standing as still as the mountains, his eyes bulging as he looked at Pick Ax aiming Tom's double-barrel at him just inside the entrance. Quicklike, the man's face went sheet white and the whole place got quiet.

"Sonny, I seen more men die than I care to tell tales about," Pick Ax said, "but iff'n you make one move with that gun, you ain't never gonna find out which tale you was." There was a sudden movement at the rear of the bar as bystanders quickly moved out of the line of fire. It was hard telling now if the man with the shotgun was as speechless as the rest of the audience seemed to be or if he was playing for time, trying to think of a move. But Pick Ax wasn't giving him any edge to play with. "Don't take all day, sonny. These bones is getting old and my trigger fingers 'bout due for a axy-dent."

With that the man let go the shotgun, just as Ray Wallace pushed through the saloon door, gun drawn.

"What the hell's going on here?" he asked, taking in what must have looked like a confusing situation at best. "Pick Ax, put that thing down." I had the feeling we were all going to jail.

"Not 'til you jail this youngster, here," the old man said, not budging.

"All right, all right," the sheriff said impatiently, "just put that thing down." When Pick Ax lowered the long gun, the sheriff turned a furrowed brow to Tom, me, and the others. "Now, just what in Hades is going on here?"

"Seems to me," Pick Ax said before any of us could speak, "Tom Dobie and Finn Callahan come a-looking for a feller that cut their harness lines last night. This ugly one here's the one what did it. I seen him." Tom's face was bloodied and I felt the thickness of blood covering my upper lip, but it was our eyes that met in bewilderment at what the old-timer had just said. I figured he might try passing off the fact that the man was going for a gun against an unarmed man, which was the truth, but the story he'd just given out had stunned both Tom and me. "And if that ain't enough," Pick Ax continued, "he was about to take this Colt's to Finn's guts. That's when I stepped in."

"What about the rest of you?" the sheriff asked impatiently.

Johnstone cast a long, hard look at the man at the bar, then back at Tom and me before answering. He could easily have turned both of us in for starting the fight, but the look on his face said that he wanted to keep the whole thing private.

"Just a misunderstanding," he said, staring at the man at the bar. Then, glancing at the bartender, he added, "You got any damages, send 'em to my office and I'll pay the bill."

That seemed to be enough for Ray Wallace as he escorted the man to jail. But *my* curiosity wasn't satisfied, not one bit, and I knew Tom's wasn't either.

"He your man?" Tom asked Johnstone, wiping some blood from his face.

"Was, Dobie. Was," was all Johnstone said before leaving with his compatriots. And he didn't look any too friendly when he did. Still, you had to give him credit for being a man about it all, if nothing else.

"You always overload this thing like just now?" Pick Ax asked when we ordered drinks. "Damn thing like to broke my arm!"

"I'm surprised it didn't knock you over, old-timer," Tom grinned, sipping a beer. "I've seen toothpicks had more meat on 'em than you do."

"Did you really see that fella cut those harness lines?" I asked.

"Wellll," he said getting shy all of a sudden, "not really." Tom gave him a hard look and Pick Ax said, "But I seen him leave that shindig last night just afore it broke up. And he was heading for your cabin."

Did you ever win a fight and still feel like it was a Mexican standoff? Well, I don't know about Tom, but that's just how I was feeling as I finished that beer. The information Pick Ax had given was enough to satisfy Tom that the fight hadn't been a waste, for time was precious to him these days, especially if we were going to make a go of it in this freighting business we'd started. But somehow the blood on my lip and the bruises on my side, which I was sure would be a dark purple by the time we were back at the cabin, didn't signify the end of it.

We picked up a new set of harnesses from the maker down by the livery. Flitsch was a short, sturdy-looking man who was anything but stout. He was German and had one of the best senses of humor I'd ever run across. He wasn't what you'd call stocky, more like being put together by his Maker where it was needed and would be put to best use. He had thick forearms and callused hands and, although it was harness making he was doing now, I'd a feeling he had spent a good number of years with a hammer and anvil as well.

"Sure, Finn," he said, loading up the last of the harnesses on the mule he was lending us, "you brink her back on your next run. Sarah," he added, patting the animal, "she's gentle. I trust you and Tom mit 'er."

We took most of the afternoon getting back to the cabin, neither of us saying much, keeping our thoughts to ourselves. That Tom didn't go galloping off the way he had on the way in was understandable, for I was feeling the same pain he was, just in different places. I had made rides before where my horse was going hell-for-leather when I didn't quite feel up to it, and I'll tell you, friend, riding like that can jostle your insides like you was gut shot and dying.

We must have looked like a sad lot, walking our horses toward that cabin, for the women were standing out front by the time we pulled to a halt, both of them wearing that exasperated look women have when a man looks to be dying but ain't quite. And I'll be damned if Sam'l Dean didn't have the same look about him, too.

"See," he said to the women, pointing at Tom and me, "I told you they'd get in trouble."

"Horse apples," was all Tom said in that frustrated manner of his that told anyone who knew him he didn't want to be bothered.

Me, I fumbled around with the part of my face that didn't feel right and tried to smile as I looked down at Tally.

"Told ya everything'd be all right."

Chapter 6

"Ouch!" Tom said, flinching as he spoke. "You ain't putting sauce on no side of beef, you know!"

We were both sitting at the table, shirts off, the women doing their best to patch up our bruises as we told them what had happened. As it turned out, Tom had a couple of fair-size welts on his side and back his own self, which didn't make me feel all that bad about my own. But the women weren't too keen on them, I can tell you that.

"Oh, I don't know," Lisa said, again touching Tom's side and causing him to flinch, "I've seen some steers that had more sense than you seem to have."

"Thanks," Tom said over his shoulder, sounding none too thankful as he spoke. Then, looking across the table at me, he added, "Next time I get this way I'm gonna take a bottle and head for high ground 'til I heal up right."

"Do you have any more liniment, Lisa?" Tally asked. So far she'd been quiet about the whole incident.

"There's a bottle back in my room," I said. "Sitting in the corner I think. It'll do."

Tally disappeared for a minute and was back with one of those thick brown whiskey bottles that are found in the Mexican southwest.

"You don't mean this, do you?" she said with an odd look on her face. "This looks like a—"

"Whiskey bottle." I nodded. "Yup, that's it."

"But . . . whiskey?" She frowned, holding the bottle at arm's length as though inspecting it.

"Nathan gave me the bottle when we left to come out here. Seems he got it from some fella down in Mexico when some Comancheros had taken Ellie and James. The man got killed and Nathan took a few bottles of what he had left." I smiled to myself, remembering my brother's story. "Said he tried drinking it, but never could. Only use he found for it was for medicinal purposes."

Tally uncorked the bottle and took a whiff, her eyes beginning to water. "I'll say! This stuff would take the paint off a riverboat's deck!"

Lisa and Tom laughed, but I sure did feel better when she dabbed some on my side. It had a cooling effect at first, then seemed to set my side afire, much, I imagined, as it would a man's stomach.

We ate shortly afterward, Pick Ax taking seconds on just about everything he could. Watching him put that much food away, I got to wondering just how a man with so few teeth could eat so much.

"You get those harnesses fixed?" Tom asked Dean. "Seems like Pick Ax was only an hour or so behind us." Then, cocking a curious eye at the other, he said, "You stick around to help Dean with those harnesses? You gotta pull your weight, you work with me."

"Oh, sure," Pick Ax said brightly. "You get a couple of old coots like us on it and, shoot, why we can do stuff like that in our sleep." Then, casting an eye at Sam'l Dean, he added, "Fact is I suspicion he *was* sleeping through it."

Everyone but Dean thought it funny. Then we fell into silence again.

"Least I can read," Sam'l finally said. "Ain't that right, Tally?"

Tally nodded.

"Believe it or not, Finn," she said, "I actually got Samuel interested in one of your books this afternoon. A book of short stories, I believe it was."

"Yeah," Dean said with half a mouthful of food,

stabbing his fork as he spoke. "That Poe feller, that was him."

"Good," I said. "I think you'll like him."

"I don't know, Finn. He sure can tell some scary tales."

Of that I was sure. The man had gained a reputation in his own time as a genius writer, and I had read most of his works. The only sad part was the news that had come out here not long ago that Poe had drunk himself to death the year before. He would be missed, but I knew that his stories, criticisms, and poems would be read for some time to come. That he could pull his readers into a story effectively was evident by the fact that I could hardly remember ever seeing Sam'l Dean reading a book before this.

Tally had turned out to be a better cook than I had expected. She and Lisa poured more coffee for us men and set out a plate of the "bear sign" that they had worked on that day. Even Tom, as crotchety as he seemed, paid Tally a compliment on the doughnuts.

After we'd had our fill, Tom and I walked outside to finish off our coffee. One of the things I had liked about the placement of our cabin was the cool breeze that inevitably came by at night. It took the sun just a big longer to set where we were located and I liked that, for it gave a body just that much more of the day to appreciate what he had. And I had plenty, that was for sure. I was watching the horizon turn a rusty shade of brown as I thought of Tally and what lay ahead for us, how happy I was that she had come. But the thought didn't last long when I heard Tom cussing another blue streak beside me.

"What's the matter, hoss? Side getting to you?"

"Not just that," the big man said, grimacing as he slowly moved a part of his hip that must have been stiff. "I don't know if you've given it any thought, pard, but we got a run tomorrow and I ain't too awful sure I'm gonna be too happy about making it."

"Yeah," I said, suddenly remembering our schedule and feeling the pain in my own body. "That's right. Can't put it off, either."

"That's for sure. Meeting our schedule is the only thing

we've got going for us right now, especially with these bigger outfits buying everyone out.''

And that was the truth. A man could make a small fortune off of the men who were making big fortunes out here, and you'd figure that the charges would be the main consideration. But they weren't. Oddly enough, those who were making the bigger strikes were more interested in getting the gold to the assayers office as soon as they could than the amount they had to pay for it. So staying on time was critical to us at this point.

''Got any suggestions?''

''You could send us.''

I turned around to see Pick Ax and Sam'l Dean nearing us. Tom and I gave each other a look and nodded to one another. They had heard every word we had said.

''You make a habit of sneaking up on people and listening to conversations that ain't none of your business, do you?'' Tom was talking to both of them, a bit of the meanness crawling back into his voice.

''Shoot, no!'' Pick Ax said. ''I been doing it all my life.''

''Thas right!'' Dean said, actually agreeing with Pick Ax on something. ''Afore you youngsters come along, all we had to listen to out here in the west was Injuns . . . and some of them wasn't all that sociable.''

I was tempted to laugh at the two old coots, for what they said made a bit of sense. But Tom didn't seemed too pleased with their antics.

''What's this about sending *you two*?'' He said it with a derisiveness that let the two old men know right off what he thought of their idea.

''Well, that way you could rest up,'' Pick Ax said. ''Me'n Sam'l here could take the run for you.''

''Oh, no,'' Tom said, letting out a vehement protest that only slowed to a grimace when he tried to gesture with his left arm.

''Don't trust us, huh!'' Dean could be accusatory and do it well when he wanted to, and right now he wanted to.

''It's not that,'' I said, breaking in before Tom could hurt himself anymore. I wasn't about to tell them that Tom was the kind of man who wanted to get things done by himself, with or without anyone's assistance. "Look, it's just that . . . you don't know the contact men we have to deal with." I said it grasping at straws, hoping that these two old-timers wouldn't catch it.

"Yeah, that's right." The way Tom said it I had the feeling that if he could have wiped the sweat from his brow right then and there, he would have.

"I still say they don't trust us," Dean said to Pick Ax.

"Look," Tom said, "I'll think on it tonight. All right?"

"All right, but—"

"I'll think on it."

The sun was just breaking through as we worked on our rigs. I had a notion that Tom hadn't slept all that well the night before. Me, I had laid down on my good side and hadn't woken up until I felt Tom's hand on my shoulder, nudging me awake. I do believe Tally could have crawled into bed right next to me and I wouldn't have been able to do anything, I was that tired. But Tom was acting as though he was going to regret this day from start to finish. He had the mood and look of a grizzly bear about him, and I doubted that it would change much before can't see.

"How well can you ride?" he finally asked without looking at me.

"Well enough," I said. "I'm gonna be sore for a while yet, so I might as well get used to it, I reckon."

"That Johnstone's stronger than I figured. Hit me across the back with a chair, and I don't mind telling you it's killing me."

"What about Pick Ax and Dean?"

"Gave it some thought. Don't think I could stand that wagon today, so I'll give 'em their wish." For a moment I felt a sigh of relief in me, thinking that I'd have the day to myself. But it wasn't to be as Tom gave me a hard look. "But we're going with 'em." When I gave him a curious look he said, "That lead's been skittish of late, and I ain't for sure that these two old coots can handle that animal when it takes a mind of its own!"

"Sounds good," I said, finishing up with my rigs. Then, glancing at Tom I half smiled. "Let's just hope *they* believe it." I knew good and well the reason Tom had given wasn't the real one, and now he knew that I knew, too.

Those old-timers were as thrilled as a kid with a new toy or, in this case, an old toy they'd been away from too long. If they didn't believe the reasoning Tom gave them for making his decision to come along, they didn't seem to care either. When they got up on the box I think Tom was expecting them to start an argument over who was going to drive and who would ride shotgun as much as I was, but to our surprise they took their places right away, Sam'l Dean on the right holding the reins, Pick Ax on the left with his shotgun. It must have thrown Tom, for he gave me a long, hard look that turned into a frown, the kind that says you're distrustful of what's going on. But then, that was Tom's way at times.

Dean and Pick Ax took off at a lively pace, and I do believe they would have gone a hell of a lot faster if they had any doubt that Tom would jerk them off the seat in a minute for mistreating the team that way. Tom didn't say much as the two drove nearly a half-mile to our front, then slowed down to a leisurely pace so Tom and I could keep them in sight. They were waiting for us down at the diggings and had the ore half loaded by the time we walked our mounts into camp. It was more than we usually took on, but I had no doubt we'd make it to our destination without any problems.

The morning went well, and we were better than halfway there when we came on some of those tricky trails that weave in and out of the side brush in those places where there is any. There was a small, hilly area off to the left as we passed, or maybe I should say as the wagon passed. Tom and I were still riding some distance behind Dean and Pick Ax, and I'll tell you, hoss, that may be the only time I was ever glad to have been shagging a ride like that, for it saved our bacon!

There were six of them and they struck like lightning! We were riding along nice and easy, and all of a sudden they were there! They were maybe a hundred yards ahead of us, and whoever it was that was pulling the holdup hadn't noticed us, not yet. Tom and I pulled up as one and I heard one of the gang yell, ''Throw 'em up!'' Tom had that Colt's revolving shotgun with him and must have been feeling game enough to take them on all by himself, for he threw me a glance and was about to slap his reins to his horse when I caught his hand in my own.

''Not yet,'' I said as quiet as I could.

He threw me another hard stare that said I was interfering with him, but I ignored it and slid off my mount. So far Pick Ax still had that shotgun cradled over his left arm and, as much as he and Dean wanted to prove themselves, I had the feeling that neither of them planned on giving up without a fight. What they needed was a diversion of some kind, and that was what I aimed on giving them. The only trouble was that I didn't have my Hawken just then. With it I could have picked one of the outlaws right out of his saddle and that would have been just what our new employees needed. Still, a man learns to make do with what he has, and what I had then was the Colt Dragoon on my hip. I'd heard tell of a man who'd killed some game with a Dragoon at some distance, but figured it for one of those tall stories you hear around camp. Yet, right now seemed to be about as good a time as any to find out how accurate the story and my Colt's were. So I pulled it out and aimed higher than any man ought to have to to hit his target and squeezed off a shot.

''Now, Tom,'' I said, throwing a leg over my own saddle as Tom charged ahead. It was no time to wait to see if I'd hit anything, and as I heard the blast of the shotgun and some pistols being fired along with it, I wasn't really all that concerned about it. If that shot of mine had hit one of them, fine, but if it made their horses skittish, well, that was all right too.

Pick Ax was right, Tom did overload that scattergun of his, for all I could see riding up there was horses milling around in a cloud of black smoke. At first I thought Tom would be firing his shotgun as well, but knew right away that if he did, he'd endanger Dean and Pick Ax. In a way that black powder charge and the confusion it had caused was just what Tom and I needed, for the outlaws didn't see us until they heard us, and then it was too late. While they were shooting at where we'd just been, both of us had slid off our horses and were adding to the cloud of black smoke. Tom took down a horse with his shotgun, but the rider scurried off and was on the back of one of his cohort's mounts in an instant. I pulled a snap shot at one of them but missed. The way his horse jumped, I must have hit the saddle at least.

The strangest damn thing happened just then! The highwaymen had failed to accomplish their objective and were in rout as I ran closer to the wagon. It was then I saw part of the face of one of the gang members, perhaps the leader, and for one instant I froze. Not more than a second, mind you, but in that time my eyes met his and I felt a shiver go down my spine. Then he turned tail and was on his way with the rest of them. I never was much on backshooting, but when people are trying to kill you you sort of throw away the rule book. So I took aim with both hands and shot one of them out of the saddle, not twenty-five yards off.

Then they were gone. Or at least three of them were.

The one I had shot was the only hit I'd made in the whole fracas. Tom had peppered the side of one of the ones who had gotten away, for I'd seen blood soaking through his pants leg. As I had suspected, the blast from Pick Ax's shotgun had blown a hole in another of the bandits and, although I hadn't heard him in all the confusion, apparently Sam'l Dean had downed another.

It was then that I saw Pick Ax slumped over in the seat next to Dean. By the time I had gotten to the side of the wagon, Dean had put his pistol in his lap and was inspecting the skinny old man.

"Damn it, hoss, you sure ain't nothing to hide behind," Dean said, inspecting the wound that appeared to be high in Pick Ax's chest. I noticed that Dean was bleeding some from his shooting arm as well. His partner was unconscious, but Dean kept right on cussing Pick Ax as though he heard every word.

I tore part of the shirt off one of the dead men, a part that hadn't been bloodied yet, and wiped away some of the blood around Pick Ax's wound. In the meantime, Tom had gathered the horses and was putting together some deadwood. One thing you learn about a man when you partner with him long enough, and that is how to think like he does, and Tom and I knew how each other thought. Oh, we had a contract to deliver our freight on time all right, but that didn't mean diddly squat when it came to saving a man's life. And you can bet those high and mighty money men who hired us wouldn't say a damn thing when we got there a tad late, for they knew how we felt about such things.

We laid him on the ground not far from the fire and, placing my bowie knife at the edge of the heat, I was glad Lisa had gone to that medical school back east. She had brought back some interesting techniques about surgery and treating wounds and such, and now they were coming in right handy. Tom had a jug of home brew that he had somehow tied in the wagon under the seat, and it came in handy, too. I took a swig to calm me before we started cutting away at Pick Ax and remembered the pain in my own body as the liquid heated up my innards. I don't know how long we were there, but it seemed like hours before I finally fished out the slug old Pick Ax had taken. That always seemed like the easy part when you knew what you had to do next. Tom held down Pick Ax by the legs and Sam'l Dean straddled his chest while I poured a slosh of that whiskey on the open wound and laid that bowie fresh out of the fire against it. The stench was awful and I found out that Pick Ax had more voice than I had given him credit for. Then he passed out and we bandaged him as proper as we could.

It was late afternoon when we got into town, two hours past our due time. But, as with every other holdup, everyone wanted to know what had happened and who it was; and, like every band of men who had come in before us, we were more dead tired than we were talkative.

"What happened?" Ray Wallace asked, as one man went for a doctor. But the sheriff was going to have to wait for his answer as Tom and I eyed the stuffed shirt who came out of the assaying office with one of those serious looks a school teacher will give a pupil. He walked over to the wagon, oblivious of the crowd or what it had gathered for, his eyebrows shooting upward as he saw Pick Ax laying on top of the load of ore.

"It's all there, Appleby," I said in a hard way. I was hoping he noticed the hatred in it, too, for I held a deep contempt for his kind of man, no matter where they lived. "All we lost was a man."

"Is he—" he started to say in that blustery fashion of his type.

"No." Tom was easily as mad as me.

"Of course, I'll pay for the doctor," he muttered, a bit of fear taking hold of him.

"Mister," I said between grit teeth, "you can't pay enough for what we lost in a man like him."

"But, isn't he the one who came in on the stage the other day? When it was robbed?"

"That's a fact," Tom said.

"It's just too damn bad a man like that's gotta come as close as this to dying to have to prove his worth." Appleby wasn't the stage depot manager who had cussed out Pick Ax the day Tally's stage had arrived, but he was cut from the same cloth, and I'll tell you, hoss, right then I was taking a serious notion to taking him apart at the seams.

"Best thing you could do right now, friend," I said "is get the hell out of my sight and have your men unload this stuff."

Big business may have had a place on the frontier in places like the mining camps, but the back east blowhards like this fella sure didn't belong here. They only seemed to function well at giving orders that others carried out for them. But stand up to them face to face and they backed off, just like Appleby was doing now.

Dean accompanied Pick Ax to the doctor's office while Tom and I went to Sheriff Wallace's office and gave him the details on the attempted holdup. A couple of Wallace's men had led away the horses with the dead man across them, and it wasn't until we had told our story that I remembered.

"Do me a favor, Ray."

"Sure, Finn. What is it?"

"Tom and I are gonna head back to the cabin when we leave here. And I'd bet even money that Sam'l Dean is gonna stick around at the doctor's as long as Pick Ax is there."

"So?"

"How about having one of your men take a look-see at the brands on those horses. We'll be back in town tomorrow to pick up the wagon and you can tell us then."

"You looking for brands that are familiar? Something from this area?" he asked, sounding a bit confused.

"I'm not sure," I said, remembering that one instant in which I'd spied the leader on his horse. "But something ain't like it's supposed to be."

Ray chuckled. "It never is with a holdup."

"That's for sure," Tom said, getting up.

"None of us recognized any of those dead men, but maybe your men might."

"Could be," he shrugged, escorting us to the door. "I'll check the wanteds and let you know in the morning."

"Thanks, Ray."

I was right about Sam'l Dean. The doctor had changed the bandage and done a better job of patching up Pick Ax than we had, but said it was best that Pick Ax remain in bed for a while. So Dean had volunteered to stand watch that night.

"How did you know Dean was gonna stay?" Tom asked as we mounted our horses to leave.

"That's something I learned from you," I said, smiling for the first time in what seemed like a long time.

"From *me*?" Tom said, frowning.

"Sure. Anyone cusses someone as much as Dean does Pick Ax has *got* to like him." When Tom's brow furrowed in a frown, I smiled again. "It's the same thing you do to your horses, ain't it?"

He shook his head slowly and smiled.

"Go to hell, Callahan."

"No thanks, hoss. What we been through today was too close to the real thing."

Then we rode home.

Chapter 7

It was after dark when we got back to the cabin, and we caught hail columbia for it from the women. But once they got through chewing us out and heard we'd been through a holdup, well, they got real interested in it, especially where Pick Ax and Sam'l Dean were.

Women fret. And that's a fact. You've never seen two women more worried about what had happened to a couple of old-timers, even though their own husband and husband-to-be were standing there before them having gone through the same ordeal. Lisa said she didn't like the comparison, but between you and me, hoss, these women were acting about as protective as a she-bear toward newborn cubs or a mare toward a colt that was still stumbling around trying to find its footing. Trouble was these two old coots might be stumbling around, but it wasn't for being newborn, that was for sure! I reckon women figure they got to take care of the old ones, for what they've done or some such notion. You can bet I didn't ponder on it much, for thinking about women is bothersome, hoss, it really is. Nathan claimed that trying to figure out a woman was a cross between figuring out how a fox thinks or which way an Indian is going to jump when you're trying to do each other in . . . you just can't tell. And it'd drive you mad trying to figure it out. The way I'd put it, women are sort of like the frontier. There's times you can't live with them for the trouble they can be,

but when you think of all the beauty they have to offer and
the kind of life they could give you, well, hoss, you can't
live without them either. That pretty well described how I
felt about this land I'd been roaming for the past fifteen
years and how I felt about Tally. Yep, the frontier and
women were pretty much alike when you thought about. Except for one thing and I reckon that's one thing about women
that you never could change. Like I said, women fret.

Lisa and Tally hurried us up through breakfast the next
morning and would have had us all riding hell-for-leather
into town if Tom and I hadn't spoken up as we mounted up.

"You just hold up there, a minute, woman," Tom said,
grabbing Lisa's reins. She looked about ready to dig her
heels into her mount. When she frowned at him in a disappointed sort of way, he said, "The town ain't going nowhere."

"Neither are Sam'l and Pick Ax," I said to both her and
Tally. "That doctor said Pick Ax needs a good bit of bed
rest, and you can bet old Dean ain't gonna let him get it
when he sees us riding in."

"And how do you know that?" Tally asked with a hint of
arrogance.

"Because those two like each other too much not to carry
on like they were gonna settle the Hundred Years War with
each other when anyone is around to see 'em."

She made a face that said she wasn't quite certain what the
words I'd spoken meant, but they were enough to calm her
down some as we headed for town. I figured it would take
her a while but she'd learn. When I first met her in New Orleans, I was wearing a greasy pair of buckskins that were
about ready to fall off of me from wear. And Tally, well,
she was dressed up right pretty in one of those fancy dresses,
which was only proper, I reckon, for she was eating in one
of them fancy eateries. The first comment she made to me
was about how surprised she was that a man in buckskins
could quote Plato. I'd straightened her out on that, and now
that she was out here she'd find out how right I was. Hell,
when she found out that Old Gabe, Old Jim Bridger, had
swapped a yoke of oxen on the Oregon Trail a few years

back for a complete set of Shakespeare, why, she'd learn just how much value we put on books out here. We didn't go around spouting off quotes from the Bard, like Bridger did, mixed in, of course, with his own Indian and mountain oaths; hell, he wouldn't be Bridger if he didn't! But that didn't mean those of us who'd spent the better share of our lives west of the Mississippi hadn't learned something from such scholarly books. Old Will, he had that one line about discretion being the better part of valor. Well, hoss, I can't prove it, you understand, but out here we just say that sometimes it is better to pull your freight than pull your gun, and to me that's the same as what Shakespeare said. Yeah, it wouldn't take Tally long to learn. Right now, though, she and Lisa were practicing one thing I found out women enjoy long before I ever met Tally, and that was ribbing their menfolk.

"One thing about men, Tally," Lisa said. She and Tally rode side by side a few yards ahead of us, and from her tone of voice she was speaking just loud enough for Tom and me to hear.

"What's that?"

"They all know what's important in life."

"Oh? Do tell." Tom gave me a suspicious look as Tally spoke in what I recognized as her best New Orleans lady's voice. You know the kind, the one with feigned surprise that is said just loud enough to be overheard . . . on purpose.

"Why, sure. And it's something you'd better get used to," she said, glancing nonchalantly over her shoulder at Tom and me. "You see, I thought my grandmother was just funning me when I was a child, but after being with Tom this long, I think she was serious."

"Really? What did she tell you?" If Tally was putting on an act, it was a convincing one, for she surely looked interested in what Lisa had to say.

"When I was a little girl she used to tell me how my grandfather had gone off to fight the Revolutionary War with Washington and all the other generals. That didn't seem so out of the ordinary, because a lot of men went off to war." Then, over her shoulder, she looked directly at us when she said, "Men are *ALWAYS* volunteering to go off to war." If there was a point to be made, it was well taken, for in a way I reckon it was Nathan and I who were to blame for getting Tom to follow us when he quit his job as a stagecoach driver, just after he and Lisa first met. It was 1846 when the war had just begun, and we left Saint Louis with some volunteers who were on their way to fight the Mexicans.

"But why did you think your grandmother was funning you?" Tally asked.

Lisa smiled, remembering the event, I was sure.

"Because," she said, still smiling, "those volunteers my grandfather was with only had six-month hitches. It was summertime, according to grandmother, and the fighting hadn't been all that fierce or that far away. So when my grandfather's hitch was up, my grandmother went after him." She laughed now, and I knew the joke was coming, although I hadn't heard this story before and it had my attention as much as Tally's.

"What was so funny?"

Lisa looked at Tally, getting her laughter under control.

"My grandmother got some of the neighbor ladies who also had husbands whose hitches were up. They went into camp and found the men all in a group, just as they suspected, and demanded that they come home because it was harvest time. You have to understand, now, that these men were in rags and several of them, including my grandfather, were shot up some and complaining something fierce." The laughter was gone from her voice now, and I thought I saw a look of disappointment come to her face as she continued the story. "Oh, yes, Tally, men know what's important in life."

"Why do you say that?"

"Because as shot up as they were and miserable and everything else, those men all told their wives to go home and harvest the crops themselves. They had all signed up for six more months. You see, they were having too much fun fighting a war." She said that last as a deliberate dig at Tom, a burr under his saddle.

"She forgot to tell you something, Tally," Tom said in a hard voice as he rode up beside the two. "If I hadn't volunteered, she'd never have wound up with me." Then, looking from Tally to Lisa, he said, "How's that for the last word?"

Lisa turned a shade of red that reminded me of the color a poker takes on when a blacksmith is stirring the coals of his fire. She glared at Tom and said "Men!" before laying the reins to her horse and galloping on.

"Damn right!" Tom yelled and took off after her.

Tally smiled as we watched the two ride out ahead of us, Tom trying to catch up with his wife, apparently not as worried about how his side was paining him as much as his pride.

"I suppose you have a last word on that subject, too?" she asked as I pulled up next to her.

"Matter of fact, I do. Way I figure it, if I hadn't done the volunteering I did, I'd never have met you during that war."

Then I leaned over and kissed her on the cheek.

Tally and Lisa were pretty much silent when we walked into the room where Sam'l Dean sat next to Pick Ax. The thin man had a sling holding his left arm in place, with a thick wad of cloth bandages wrapped around his chest and shoulder. Dean had the look of a man who had stayed up all night and was ready for some relief.

"I hear I owe you my life," Pick Ax said to me, showing a toothless smile. Seeing that was enough to convince me that he would make it.

"Not me so much as Lisa, here." When a puzzled look came to his face, I looked at Lisa and said, "She's the one who took all those doctoring lessons back east and told me about 'em. Otherwise, the way that bullet was stuck in you, I'd likely have butchered you worse than I did my first deer."

For a moment Pick Ax paled at the thought of what I had just described, then regained his composure enough to reach out with his good hand to take Lisa's in his own and kiss it as if she were some kind of royalty.

"I'm obliged to you, ma'am."

"I'm flattered," Lisa said, and the way she was blushing, I do believe she was.

"Finn, didn't you say you had somplace to go?" Tally asked as polite as you please. I figured that she and Lisa were going to fawn over Pick Ax while Tom and I took care of our business, but there was something else I had to find out before we could leave.

"In a minute, Tally." Then, turning to Pick Ax, I asked, "Did you recognize any of those men who hit us yesterday? Sam'l hasn't been out here that long, but I figured since you have you might have seen 'em before."

Pick Ax frowned. "No, can't say as I did. Things were going on pretty quick just then, and I was more concerned with seeing 'em face down than I was face up."

"Just wanted to check," I said. "Tom and I are gonna stop by Ray Wallace's office to see what he's found out."

"Hope you run into some luck."

"Hoss," Tom said, "out here, people make their own luck." He said it as a matter of fact, but we all knew it would take a lot of hard work before we'd uncover the identities of those highwaymen.

"Sam'l, why don't you come with us," I said. "You look like you could use a drink and a good meal."

The man perked right up at that prospect and followed us to the sheriff's office. Apparently, he thought we would be heading straight for the saloon, and the expression of disappointment on his face showed it.

"Ray," I said as we entered his office, "how about a cup of your coffee?"

Wallace shrugged noncommitally. "Sure, if you're game."

He handed me a cup, and I passed it to Dean, who took it with a strange look on his face.

"You said you was gonna give me a drink."

"That's it," I said, nodding toward the cup. The old-timer gave a cautious look at the dark, thick liquid and took a quick gulp. I didn't have the heart to tell him that Ray Wallace was a fine lawman but likely the worst coffee brewer

I'd ever run across, but the look of shock on Dean's face now said that he knew it all as his eyes appeared ready to pop out.

"That is gamey," he said in a whisper. You'd have sworn he had just taken his first slug of Aged-In-the-Keg Busthead.

"See, woke you right up," Tom said.

"Find anything out, Ray?"

"Not much, I'm afraid." The sheriff shuffled some of the papers on his desk, either looking for something in particular or stalling for time. He did that once in a while. But then he pulled out a sheet of paper and handed it to me. "That's the brand on those horses you were wanting. A Circle E. Recognize it?"

"No," I said. Tom shook his head too.

"Neither do I," Ray said. "It's not from any brand I've ever seen around here. None of my men have seen it before either."

"What about the outlaws themselves?" Tom asked.

"Not much there, either. One of my men used to work for a miner six, eight months back and says he recognized one of them from a holdup then, but the other two are newcomers to this game, at least out here."

"But all three horses had the same brand?" I asked.

"Yeah, that's the queer part," Wallace said, rubbing his jaw. "The horses and their brands aren't familiar at all. Only thing I can figure is they were furnished by these newcomers."

"Say," Dean said, speaking up for the first time since he'd recovered from the coffee, "now that sounds exciting." He said it with an enthusiasm I'd not heard in him before. From my experience with him down in New Orleans when I first met Tally, he was cautious about trouble, not particularly wanting to get involved if he didn't have to. It was enough to make me wonder if Ray Wallace hadn't made his coffee just a mite too strong today.

"You know something we don't?" I asked.

"No," Dean shrugged, "but this sounds like something

that Poe feller would write about. See, he's got these fellers who do, what do you call it, deee-tective work.''

Tom wasn't much of a reader and frowned at what Sam'l Dean was saying, but I had read what I could get my hands on of Edgar Allan Poe and knew what Dean was spouting off about. The man had introduced a new type of short story that wasn't anything like what Cooper or the others had written. There was someone representing good and evil, one each, in Poe's tales, and he took the reader right along with the narrator of the story to discover just who the evil-doer was. It made great reading, but I had my own problems to deal with, and Tom said it as well as I could have.

"Hell, Dean," he said, sounding mad, "there's people out there trying to kill us and you want to talk about some book?!" Glancing back and forth between Dean and the sheriff, I could tell that Tom wasn't any too pleased with what Ray Wallace had told us either. "Finn, I got a feeling this is gonna be one of those days." Then he stomped out.

"Some day that temper of his is gonna get him in trouble, Finn," Ray said.

"It already has, Ray," I said without telling him about what had taken place with Lisa on the ride in this morning. "It already has."

Ray Wallace had nothing else in the way of information for us that pertained to the hold up, so I took Sam'l Dean to one of the eateries for the promised meal. Besides, it was getting on toward noon and I figured the women were going to spend as much time as they could pampering Pick Ax, so I ordered some grub for my own self as well. You'd have thought Dean hadn't eaten in a week the way he put that food away. My own meal was tasteless, and I wound up giving the better share of it to Dean, who readily ate every morsel of it, too. If I didn't act as starved as Sam'l, perhaps it was because I had something else churning around in my belly that needed settling before I'd eat proper.

All hell seemed to have broken loose since right before Tally got off that stagecoach a few days back, and none of it made any sense. Here Tom and I had a decent business going and all of a sudden we were being sabotaged and told

we had to sell to some almighty bigger outfit and being shot
at for good measure. I could accept the element of danger involved in our business as far as being held up went. Hell,
there were enough men who died in the mines or were
bushwacked for a day's earnings at a creek bed not to make
daily death and the threat of it an ordinary part of surviving
out here. And it was true that the Adams Express Company
was buying out as many independents as it could, for such
talk had been around for a while before Johnstone had approached Tom and me about our business. But the sabotage,
the cutting up of our harnesses like they were, well, that was
just too unlike them. Those bigger outfits had a reputation to
uphold, and most of them did a good job of it. You had to be
able to trust whoever it was hauling your life savings to the
assayer's office in this country, at least enough to know they
weren't likely to ride off with your hard-earned findings. So
integrity was something that a good, honest businessman
paid even more attention to than advertising his product.
And so it seemed unlikely that the Adams Express people
had anything to do with those harnesses being cut to rib-
bons. True, Johnstone was more of a bully than an agent,
but he worked for the Adams company and must have had
something worth being hired for . . .

"Ever hear of Alexander Majors?" Dean said, inter-
rupting my line of thought.

"Sure. Did some hauling during and after the Mexican
War, if I recall right. Why?"

"Well, I never met the man, but if what I heard is true,
he's likely as good with them hosses as your partner Dobie
is."

"And?" I gave him a curious look, unsure of what he was
getting at.

"If he's in the area, why'nt you and Tom round him up
and see if can he give you a hand?"

"I doubt it," I said. "Last I heard, he was operating out
of Santa Fe or the Kansas Territory, one. Besides, why do
you think we're needing help?"

"Cause I don't think your Dobie friend has got much use

for me or Pick Ax or our likes," Dean said, getting some of
the venom out of his system.

"I wouldn't judge him that harshly, Sam'l. Tom's a bear
of a man and, like it or not, acts like one at times. It's not
one of his better qualities, but I've learned to put up with
it." That answer only pacified part of what was bothering
him though, for he still had a look about him that said he was
going on the warpath with my partner the next time he ran
into him.

"Look, Sam'l, if it's about yesterday and having you two
ride, it wasn't that Tom didn't trust you at all. It's just that
he's got a special feel for our teams, whether it's the horses,
mules, oxen, take your pick. I reckon he's as jealous of his
animals as some men are their women or as my brother is his
guns. It's just one of those traits that you accept in a man." I
rose, getting ready to leave. "And Sam'l."

"Yeah."

"The more people you can get along with out here, the
better."

I tossed a coin on the table to pay for the meal and left, not
caring whether he joined me or not. So far all I'd had contact
with was people who wound up looking for a fight. Well, I
had more and better things to do than try and pacify everyone I met that day. Heading back for the doctor's office, I
hoped I would have better luck with the women. I knew Pick
Ax would be in good spirits with all the attention he was getting. But that seemed like the only sure bet.

I was right. Tally had wrapped some bear sign in a cloth
and brought it in, and the two were feeding Pick Ax as much
of it as he could down with some of the doctor's coffee.

"You keep feeding him like that and he's gonna put on
enough weight in no time to get back to driving that rig of
ours," I said, taking in the scene. Like I said, women fret,
and those two must have been treating Pick Ax like he'd
only live out the day.

"Shoot, boy," the old-timer said, "I'm ready to go
now."

He was propped up in bed and was about to make a move
to get out when he must have realized that he was only cov-

ered by the sheet from the waist down and likely didn't have a stitch of clothing on!

"Well, almost," he added shyly.

The women gave their own shy little titters and turned a light shade of pink at the same time Pick Ax did.

I went over what I had found out with them and waited for the doctor to return from a call he had to make. Pick Ax was serious about wanting to get going, although I wasn't sure if it was because he couldn't stand being cramped in this or if he couldn't stand the thought of having Sam'l Dean babysit him another night. I got the feeling it was a bit of both and hoped Tom, in all his anger, had remembered to claim our wagon, for it too was something we needed to pick up in town.

"What do you think, doc?" I asked a short while later when the physician returned. "Can you turn him loose?"

"He'd better!" Pick Ax said, and I had the feeling I was gonna have another fighter on my hands. "I ain't a-staying here no longer than I have to!"

"That sounds like a firm indictment," the doctor said. He wasn't any too unhealthful his own self by his looks. He was what they called robust-looking back east, and in some of those books I'd read. But he being in the profession he was, I'd say "healthy" was the best word to describe him. I wouldn't want to say he hadn't seen his feet in a while, but I doubted if anyone other than Pick Ax could fit through a double door with him at the same time. If you get my drift. When Pick Ax gave him a confused look, the doctor added, "It means you're getting better."

"I'd want to get rid of someone who complained as much as Pick Ax, too," Sam'l Dean said, coming through the doorway.

"Normally, I would recommend another day or two of bed rest," the doctor continued. "But since our patient seems to be healing rather rapidly out of sheer will, I'll turn him over to you, Mrs. Dobie, if you're willing to take the responsibility." Pick Ax was about to shoot his good arm out into the air and let out one of his yells when the doctor's hand fell over his mouth like a clamp. "I'd not advise you to do that, sir, unless you've a desire to rupture something else inside you.''

"I can take care of him,'' Lisa said as Pick Ax's eyes bulged out and then formed a look of relief all at once.

The doctor gave Lisa some kind of medicine for Pick Ax to take with the admonition that if the patient failed to take it, Lisa had better think up some sort of punishment for him right quick, all of which meant that the stuff likely smelled and tasted like castor oil.

"Oh, he'll take it,'' Tally assured the doctor, ''or I won't make any more of that bear sign for him.'' With that a hopeless look came over Pick Ax's face, and the man knew he was doomed.

Tom had pulled up front with the wagon, and Dean and I helped Pick Ax out to it once he had gotten dressed. He still wore the same trousers, but his shirt had been destroyed by the gunshot wound and the blood, and the one he wore now dwarfed his frail body. I do believe that if I hadn't seen the skin-and-bones man sitting up in bed before, I'd have thought he was some sort of skeleton that had been taken from a funeral parlor.

Dean got up on the box, his hands on the brake release, ready to go, when the women came out of the doctor's office. Tally and I were saying our good-byes to the doctor when it happened.

I turned on the boardwalk to get my horse and there she was!

"Oh, hi, sugar,'' she said just as sweet as can be and then kissed me. It was the same one who'd pulled this stunt before, and as much as I tried to pull away from her, she wasn't letting me.

"What the hell!'' I heard Tally yell and, somewhere in the background, Tom started to laugh.

"I just wanted to thank you for showing me such a good time yesterday afternoon,'' the woman said with a smile after she was through kissing me. I don't know how I looked, but I was feeling like a man who's been ambushed and only has a few hours of life left after getting shot out of the saddle. I wanted to grab hold of her and shake the truth from her, but the shock of having this happen to me a second time was something I'd never experienced before, and she was gone as quickly as she had appered.

"You can't believe—" I stuttered to Tally. But I didn't get much of an answer; or, at least, what I did get was totally unexpected and not to my liking at all. Tally hit me across the face with her open hand, so hard, I thought, that the whole town must have heard the echo of it. Then she did the same with her other hand, just as hard. No man would have gotten past the first swing, if that, before I would have let him feel my own fist. But this was the woman I loved who was hitting me! Everything had been straightened out, and here she was exploding at me again. No one had ever hit me before like that and, damn it, I was just too stunned to do anything but stand there like a fool and listen to her start to cuss me as well!

"Hold on, woman!" It was Tom, and the laugh was gone from his voice as it took on a cold, hard commanding quality. "He don't deserve that! That woman was lying! You had any brains you'd be looking to beat the hell out of her, not Finn!"

"Oh, you're all liars!" Lisa yelled at her husband. "You'd take up with him just to protect him!" A viciousness had come to her voice as well as she spoke. "You probably shared the same woman!" A vein stuck out on the side of her neck as she yelled "Men!" and put the spurs to her mount. Tally had swung up in the saddle by then too and was doing the same.

"What in the hell got into them?!" I heard Tom say as he watched the two women ride out hell-for-leather. He had the same unbelieving look on his face that I must have had on mine; that of a man who could fight grizzly bears with one hand tied behind his back, but whose heart would break like a baby's after hearing the words he just had from the woman he loved.

"Am I missing something?" Pick Ax said, a bit perplexed himself.

"I don't know," Dean said, shaking his reins, "but if you're smart, pard, you'll keep your mouth shut. I got a feeling all four of 'em is in the mood to kill. And I don't plan on being around when the shooting starts! Hiyaah!!'' He shook the reins harder, and I watched him leave with Pick Ax in the back of the wagon.

I don't know why but we sat there, Tom and I, on our horses, watching the dust as the horses Lisa and Tally rode disappeared into the distance, followed by the wagon Dean was driving. Then we looked at one another, sort of dumblike, I reckon, each of us waiting for the other to say something.

"I ain't much of a drinker," I said, finally. "But right now I could sure use one."

"Not a drink," Tom replied. "A bottle."

Like the fella said, it had been one of those days.

And it turned out to be one of those nights.

Chapter 8

Pa always said the Lord looks after drunks and fools, but at the moment I wasn't sure just which I was. The way I was feeling I might have been both!

My head hurt and there was the taste of blood in my mouth and I was lying on my back. At least, when I opened my eyes it seemed that way. I turned my head to my side to spit out some of the blood and saw Tom. He was face down and passed out . . . or dead. There was trouble and I found myself instinctively closing my fist around what I held. But it wasn't the butt of a pistol or even a knife. It was hard wood, and it was then I focused my eyes and realized that both Tom and I were in a jail cell, if you'd want to call it that.

"I told 'em you were too hard-headed to die." The voice belonged to Ray Wallace, and he said the words in a joshing tone.

I propped myself up on an elbow, looking over my shoulder at Ray, his features still fuzzy to my eyes.

"You don't remember anything, do you?" he asked.

"No, I . . . what is there to remember?"

Tom stirred then, likely going through the same motions I just had, trying to figure where he was and why. He squinted at me, then the sheriff, his face asking the same question as mine. I sat up, but it was painful, everything on my left side feeling as if it were caved in. At first, breathing was a problem, but after a few slow, deep breaths I thought I'd survive it, whatever "it" was.

"There wasn't any room at the hotel," Ray said. "Besides, I doubt they'd have taken you, the shape you were in."

"If you're trying to be funny, you're talking to the wrong man, Ray." It was the first time I'd spoken, and the words came out kind of choppy.

"You don't remember anything? Nothing at all?"

"Likely not, Ray," Tom said, not seeming all that worse for wear. "He ain't an old-time drinker like you and me." I think he tried to smile then, or maybe it was the crooked way his face looked at the time, as though it had been rearranged.

Wallace disappeared and I looked toward the window. The sun had been up for an hour or more from what I could see. When he came back, Ray was balancing a third tin cup between the two he held. Two of them had coffee, which he set down, one cup before each of us. The third held water, which he handed first to Tom, then me.

"Get the swill outta your mouth and have a drink of coffee," he said. Then he reached around the corner and pulled a three-legged stool out and placed it beneath him. I got the notion he wanted some answers, and he didn't figure on letting us go anywhere until he got them. Or else we were sitting in on a real live war council and I was just daydreaming that there were bars for walls—which didn't seem too likely from the taste in my mouth.

"That stuff'll either settle your stomach or bring up what's left," he said, indicating the cups of coffee. "But like you told your friend yesterday, it'll wake you up for sure."

Then things started coming back to me. Riding into town and the argument Lisa and Tom had gotten into. Loading Pick Ax into the wagon. The blond woman who just happened to be there when Tally was and the argument that followed and the women riding off like Tom and I had the plague. The drinking that Tom and I had started out to do and a meal I thought I remembered eating but could only be sure I did from the acrid taste still in my mouth. My thoughts stopped for a moment and all I could see was Tally and Lisa riding off. The women!!

"Judas priest!" I said and tried to get up. I moved but six inches before feeling a pressure force me back down. At first I thought it was Ray Wallace, but he hadn't moved. If my ribs had felt bad the day before, I didn't know if I could describe the way they were feeling just then—they were that bad.

"Not so fast, Finn." The authority was coming out in Ray now, any humor he might have shown gone. "You two can leave in a bit, but first I want to know what happened to you."

"What happened to us?" The whole situation seemed confusing at best. "Hell, I can't remember anything after walking into one of those saloons."

"You're right, hoss," Tom said with a straight face. "You ain't no drinker. And damn little fun to be with. Do you know he spent all night crying in his beer over that damned woman?" he said to the sheriff. I would have gotten up to hit him if I had the strength, but I wasn't sure I did. Breathing was painful, and I wasn't in any hurry to have anyone take a look at my side, for fear of what it looked like.

"You remember?"

"Yeah," Tom said, "most of it. Seems to me I was all but carrying Finn from one saloon to another when we got shanghaied by more'n a couple of pirates."

"That sounds about right," Ray said, nodding. "The fellas that brought you in found you both in an alley under a bunch of fishnet like some drunken sailors that couldn't find their way back to their ship."

I said nothing, only listened to the conversation being carried on. But oddly enough, I felt something nudge at my mind, or what was working of it. Maybe I hadn't been as drunk as I thought and did remember some of what went on. I hadn't been joshing Tom when I told him I wasn't much of a drinker, for I never had taken to it like Nathan or Cooper Hansen or Lije Harper. It was one of those personal preferences, a choice you had to make in a land where more than one man believed that his drinking capacity was a measure of his manhood as well. I knew better than that and took the ribbing from those who gave it, although I did have a beer once in a while. But last night, well, I wasn't any too ready to go through that routine again. Not the way my head felt that morning.

"Fishnet? That what that was?" Tom shook his head, likely remembering what had happened. "Those fellas could hit awful hard. That much I do know."

"What did I do?" I asked.

Tom snorted. "Took a lot of hard punches, hoss, just like I did. Only I think you were past feeling 'em right then."

"Anybody see it?"

"Not that I've been able to find out," Ray said. "Whoever it was didn't take anything, either. I got your guns and knife out on the desk. Looks like you just got somebody god-awful mad at you. But I'll do some more asking around."

He pulled back the stool and went back to his office as Tom and I drank what we could of the coffee. The date and the day might change, but Ray Wallace's coffee never would, at least not until he found him a woman who could make it for him.

I was anxious to leave, wanting to get back to the cabin and see if the women were safe, but my body was telling me to take it easy, and having been that way before, I heeded its advice. Tom and I stumbled out to Ray's office and picked up our guns, thanking him for the coffee.

"Oh, almost forgot," he said, digging into his shirt pocket. "You must have dropped this. One of the men who brought you in said they found it near you." He handed me a solid gold piece, one of those I had found down on the Rio Grande during the Mexican War. They were larger than normal and I had gotten some awesome looks from the people I had paid with them. It was the kind of look people gave you when they just knew there had to be some kind of legend behind where that gold came from, and that there was. I stared at the gold piece for a second before pocketing it.

"Anything wrong, Finn?"

"No, Ray. Nothing. Thanks for looking after us. I'm obliged."

"Part of my job." He smiled.

"I wonder how the women and the old-timers are doing?" I asked Tom when we were outside.

"Probably doing all right," he said, shrugging noncommittally. He could put on whatever kind of tough act he wanted to for the rest of the world, but I knew Tom Dobie better than that. He was as worried as I was.

Our horses were still in front of the eatery I remembered going into the day before. We got them to a trough and watered them some before mounting. Then we walked them out of town, sort of hoping that not too many people who'd been up the night before and seen us then saw us now. Sometimes not remembering what you did can be a blessing, but the thought of someone giving me a mischievous smile and knowing more than I did about it just rattled me more than I cared to tell, so I was anxious to get out of the town.

"Tom," I said when we were finally mounted and out of there.

"Yeah."

"How often have you seen me use these since we've been out here?" I asked, pulling the gold coin out of my pocket.

He shrugged. "Not at all that I can recall. Why?"

I tossed the coin, catching it. "It's mine, all right, hoss. But you're right, I haven't carried any of these since we went into business out here."

"I don't like the look on your face, son." Tom said it as his own face began to take on a strange look.

"If I didn't have it, those fellas that took us on must have had it, and they had it—"

"They must have gotten it from out our way," Tom said, finishing my thought. "I don't know if my body can stand the ride, but I sure hope these horses can."

"It ain't the horses I'm worried about, Tom. It's the women!"

Neither of us had to do any more talking right then. I knew Tom was hurting as much as I was, but it made no difference. We both slapped the reins hard over our horses'

sides and dug in our heels. I was grimacing so hard I thought
at one point that I was going to fall off the horse. And all the
while I was thinking that someone had Tally, had Lisa, and
had killed off those old-timers while they were having their
fun with our women! It was enough to make me killing mad
and that made me forget, at least for a while, the physical
pain I was in. That kind of feeling may be the only good that
has ever come out of revenge, for it seemed as though we
rode and rode and then all of a sudden we were there. We
rode into that yard with guns drawn, ready to charge hell
with a bucket of water, put out the fire and skate on the ice!
And, damn, did I feel like a fool!

The cabin was still standing, and no one was in sight.
There was no sign of a scuffle at all, and there were Tom
and I sitting a-saddle with Dragoons in hand looking like—

"You look disappointed," Lisa said as she walked out
the door, drying a plate.

"I told you they'd come back," Tally said as she too
came out.

"Damn!" Tom said, holstering his pistol and dismount-
ing as I did the same.

"Helluva welcome, ain't it?" I said to Tom.

"Should've expected it, I reckon." The frustration was
once again growing in both of us as the two women began
acting in a superior manner, almost as if they wanted a fight.
"Any coffee in there?" Tom asked, taking a step forward.

"There's coffee," Lisa said, stepping in front of him,
"but not for you."

"That's right," Tally said in a bold manner. "You see,
we've decided that you two aren't welcome here anymore."

"What?" I think Tom and I said it both at the same time;
and loud enough to make me listen for an echo to it in the
canyon next to us.

"Not until we get an apology and an account of what you
two were doing in town last night!" Lisa said.

"You got a lot of gall," Tom said, turning beet red as he
spoke through gritted teeth.

"Well, now, children, this surely is interesting."

Sam'l Dean came walking slowly over from the barn

where he'd been working. He looked to be enjoying the scene he was seeing, a grin on his face. And I reckon that just made all of us the madder.

"What do you want?" Tom demanded.

"Well, I figured I might be able to give you youngsters a good piece of advice. But first you'd have to quiet down a bit." He was having a good time, old Dean was, and like I said, none of us was any too happy about it.

"What the hell are you talking about?" I said.

"Well, I never was much of a marriage fixer upper," he said, lowering his voice so that only the four of us could hear him. "But I done a lot of watching over the years, yessirree. And I seen all sorts of people argying and I learned me something. Yes I did." He said it emphatically, as though it were a piece of wisdom he had been holding back for just such an occasion.

"Make sense, Dean," Tom said impatiently, wanting to get on with his arguing while the mad was still in him.

"What I learned," Dean said, shaking a finger at us, "was that whenever families start to arguing, why, they ain't nobody hears what's being said . . . 'cepting the neighbors." He was smiling again, proud of his wise offering.

"Sam'l," Lisa said patiently, "who cares. I don't care if the whole world hears me." She said the last in a raised voice.

"Well, now," Dean said, his voice down to a whisper only Tom and I could catch, the seriousness coming to his face again, "a good deee-tective, like that Poe feller"—here he eyed me—"he'd notice that you got yourself a neighbor over yonder by those trees. Was he skinny as that loafer, Pick Ax, nobody'd see him, but a good deee-tective—"

I turned away from the group, walking slowly back beyond the mounts and off to the side, away from the cabin.

"Don't you walk away from me, Finn Callahan!" I heard Tally say behind me.

"Don't push it," I said, ignoring her as I continued to walk.

"What?" she said, grabbing me by the left arm and

standing in front of me. The way I was feeling I'd about
gone my limit. Here she was trying to pick a fight and standing in my line of fire, for Sam'l Dean had been right, there
was a man trying to hide behind one of our trees.

"Don't want to admit that you were seeing that woman
again!" A fire was building inside of her, that was plain to
see. Trouble was I had the feeling she was acting out some
day long gone that had nothing to do with me. If she figured
I was supposed to put up with it, she was sadly mistaken.
But she wasn't finished yet, for the fire in her eyes grew
deeper, and she brought her hand up to slap me. It pained me
to move as fast as I did, but like I said, I was getting too
damn mad to feel the pain all that much. I caught her by the
wrist, held it in midair as she struggled to pull it loose. Now
it was my turn to get angry, and I'll tell you, hoss, it wasn't
hard at all. I'd known some Comanches and Mexicans from
back in Texas who'd never gotten past pushing me as hard
as Tally was, not without getting a fistful of opinion to give
them a second thought about charging head on again.

"You sure have been getting awful righteous of late," I
said, still holding her wrist in my hand and hoping she was
getting the idea of just how fed up I was with her.

"Let go of my wrist," she said in her own mad voice.

"Sure." I said it between my teeth, but I was looking
over her shoulder as I did. The man was still there, likely
getting a bit edgy about trying to watch the arguing Tally
and I were doing and what the other three were up to as well,
and I figured that was in my favor. I didn't feel up to tack-
ling anybody right now, but I still had enough energy to pull
that Colt, and with Tally as a cover I did just that. She was
about to go spewing over at the mouth again when I let go of
her wrist . . . after I gave it a fling off to the side. She let
out a little scream as she fell to the ground, enough to get the
man's attention. But by the time he was pulling his gun
around toward me, I already had mine cocked and aimed at
him.

"Drop it!" I yelled out at him. Now, friend, you may
think that what I was doing was a bit foolish, me standing
out in the broad daylight like that and him with a tree to hide

behind, but I just flat didn't give a damn. "You want to live to see the sun set today, you'll do as I say, friend."

He could have thrown down on me but he didn't. Maybe it was the tone of my voice or maybe he saw the mad in me from that distance; maybe it was all that made him lower his six-gun. But more likely it was the sight of Tom and Dean coming at him from his blind side. Tom had his Dragoon out and a mad look about him, and Dean had the pitchfork he'd been carrying in his hand, set at his side just like he was readying to toss some hay from the loft and this fella was it!

The look on Tally's face was one of not only surprise but fury as she approached me.

"You mean you knew he was there and let me stand there like . . . like . . . some kind of target!"

"Shut up and get inside!" I said, holstering my pistol now that Dean, who seemed to be enjoying it all, got nice and close to our visitor with his pitchfork.

"You can't tell me that!" She was acting outraged, but believe me, it wasn't nothing like I was feeling.

"Don't tell me I *can't*," I said, poking her in the chest with a finger. "I just *did.*" I said it hard, like I would to any man who pushed me that way. "Now git." If it could have dropped that far, I'd wager that her chin would have some clear down to the valley that showed from the loose button on the man's shirt she wore. You know what I mean, the part of a woman that's . . . healthy. Then she spun around, a flabbergasted look on her face, and marched toward the cabin.

"Same goes for you, woman!" Tom said. He must have been in the same mood I was, for he holstered his pistol and he shot his arm out toward Lisa as though he had an imaginary pistol in his hand and was pointing it now.

"Or *what!*" The woman was still defiant. But I knew it wouldn't last long when I saw the rage build up in Tom's face.

"Or I'll take you over my knee and put so many blisters on your bottom, you'll think you was born with calluses!"

"You wouldn't!" Her defiance had changed to fear

mixed in with a goodly portion of embarrassment, I thought, as she became more cautious now.

"Don't bet against it," I heard Tom say. There was a pause, a silence in the air that could have been cut with a butter knife. And I had a feeling it was that silence just then that was having a lot to do with how Tom and Lisa would view one another from there on out. A frustrated look came to Lisa's face as she turned to the cabin and stalked off.

"Well, now," Dean said, "seeing's you got your *major* problems took care of, what about this feller?"

"Yeah, what about you?" I asked, turning my attention to the stranger. "You sure do seem to have an urge to get your nose busted." That didn't seem to bother him as much as the pitchfork old Dean had at his side. I reckon some people are like that, having their own particular fears and all, I mean.

"I was just wandering by and heard you folks arguing and got curious," the man said in a cautious manner. He had a gaunt face that looked like it might get just a wee bit gaunter before he got out of trouble he was in. If he got out of it.

"Hogwash, sonny," Dean said, "I seen you out here just afore these two rode up." He paused then, a slow grin coming to his face. "You know, boys," he said, speaking to Tom and me, but all the time looking right into the eyes of the man before us, "I recall old John Colter telling me what the Blackfeet do to their captives." The stories of Lewis and Clark and their guide, John Colter, had become as much a legend out here as Daniel Boone and his exploits, and there was even a place called Colter's Hell where the trapper had performed a somewhat gigantic feat some years back after he had been captured by hostile Indians. But that's a whole 'nother canyon. By the look in his eyes, I could see that the man had heard bits and pieces of the story himself.

"Yeah," Tom agreed, "seems I recall it too. Used to stake out their victims, wasn't it?"

"That's right," I said. "Then they'd strip them naked and pull out a razor sharp knife and take to cutting strips of their skin and peeling it back to see how brave they were.

But I forget, Sam'l, was it one-inch or two-inch strips they cut 'em into?''

"Oh, it was one-inch strips, son," Dean said and I'd swear I saw some craziness in the glint in his eyes. "Them Blackfeet's devilish mean, they is. Yessirree, they liked their fun. That they did." Then his gaze shifted to me. "Still do." The smile was gone now as Dean returned to the present. "Well," he said, calm as you please as he walked toward the barn, "I'll get the stakes."

We all of us watched him go, Tom as curious as to whether the old-timer was serious as I was. But it was the fella between us who'd gone sheet white in the face who'd been made a believer.

"He's joshing, ain't he?" The man's hands started to shake.

"I don't know," I said, watching Dean disappear into the barn. "But he's old enough to have been there when Colter was outrunning those Indians. What do you think, Tom?"

"He's coming back with four stakes," he said with conviction. "I've spent time in the mountains and I've seen that look before." I could tell by the tone in his voice that he wasn't storytelling either. "I'd get real talkative right quick if I was you, mister."

"He's got a point," I said. "Now, none of us believes that story about just passing by, so why don't you level with us before we turn you over to Sam'l?"

"You'll let me go?" The man was desperate to get away now, and I had a plan of my own coming to mind.

"Sure," I said, "just tell us what you're doing up here."

Tom wasn't much in favor of the idea but had the good sense to let me handle it my own way as he stood back and watched.

"I don't know what the reasoning is, mister, but the boss said he wanted me out here by this morning to see what would happen between you and your lady friend when you rode in."

Some of it was starting to make sense now. If what this man was saying was true, the woman in town had been a plant to make me look bad in front of Tally. And she had done a damn good job of it, for I was even having second thoughts about Tally, especially after this morning.

"And who's the boss?" Tom asked.

The man shrugged. "Mister, you ain't gonna believe this, but I don't know." I took a step toward him and he cringed in fear, backing away. "Look, I'm telling you the truth! I met the man, all right. Tall, medium big type of fella. But I ain't never seen him before and I don't know his name."

"He didn't give it?"

"Nope. Just offered me fifty dollars if I'd come out here and do like I was told and report to him."

"He ain't paying you enough," I said. Glancing over my shoulder, I saw Sam'l Dean emerge from the barn with stakes and a hammer in his hands. The sight of him struck terror in the man's eyes. "I see you around here again, friend, I'll turn you over to Sam'l there."

"Well, if you're through, mister, I can think of three different territories I'd rather be visiting right now." The closer Dean came, the more the man physically shook.

"Then git!" Tom said, and when he did I don't believe I've ever seen anyone run faster for a mount than that fella did.

"Hmph!" Dean said as he neared, watching the man ride off. "Never could understand why people never stick around for the rest of the story."

Tom glanced at me, confused. "Story?" he asked the old-timer. "What the hell you gonna do with those?" he said, indicating the four stakes Dean was carrying. A closer look revealed what must have been either blood stains or red paint on bits and pieces of the stakes. "We figured you were gonna do some practicing on that fella."

"Oh, these is some stakes I taken off'n a handful of Blackfeet back in '37. They were fixing to do some knife work on some tenderfoot that got hisself caught. Got all four of 'em, I did."

"You mean you wouldn't have used them on that fella?" I said.

"Oh, course not," Dean said with a wave of his hand. "On the other hand, if he hadn't told you what you wanted to know . . . He *did* tell you what you wanted to know, didn't he?''

"That he did," I said.

There was coffee on the table when we entered the cabin. The women didn't seem too awful happy, but Pick Ax was excited about what had taken place outside, having watched it all from the window. He thought Dean's story and actions particularly funny, a good indication that he was healing faster than I expected.

"There's a few things that have to be straightened out," I said to Lisa and Tally. At first they were reluctant to talk, but once we got started, Tom and I told them everything that had happened on our drinking spree the night before. The looks on their faces were incredulous as Tom finished telling the story, almost as though they were thinking we had made it all up.

"You just check with Ray Wallace if you don't believe us," I added. "He'll vouch for it and likely get you the two fellas that brought us in to tell you the same thing, if you like."

"You really did that?" Tally asked, her doubt turning to amazement now. "After being beat up you rode out here in that condition just to make sure we were safe?" I could tell by the tone of her voice that she was feeling a bit flattered at the whole incident. Mention of the ride had brought back the realization that my guts were still needing to settle down some and that I had more bruises than I cared to count.

"You were that worried about us?" Tally said with a hint of disbelief in her voice. "Even after yesterday and—"

"That's a fact," Tom said, finishing his coffee.

The women seemed to be a bit out of sorts at the moment; maybe speechless would be a better word. Lisa was the first one to recover.

"Tally, why don't you get the liniment and I'll pour some more coffee," Lisa said with a smile. All of a sudden everything seemed to be right in the world for her and Tom.

When Tally returned, she set the medicinals on the table as I stood up. She had a look on her face that was supposed to be a combination of shame and humility, I reckon, but just then I had a few things on my mind that needed saying as well.

"I suppose I should apologize," she said, smiling weakly.

"I suppose you could," I said, looking down at her, a frown coming to my face as the anger I'd been feeling got ready to come out. "You know, there was a time I could look at you and that smile of yours would make me laugh inside because I'd never seen one like it before . . . never wanted to see another one again. But you've changed, Tally. Somewhere between then and now you've changed. I don't know how or why or what made the difference, but I sure don't care for it. Not one bit.

"The way you've been acting the last couple of days, you'd think you own me or something. And I'll tell you something, Tally. As pushy as you are, there ain't a man out here'd put up with you. Well, no one ever owned me and no one ever will, so you'd better get used to being lonely out here or head back east, where you belong, because you sure don't fit in here."

The realization of what she had done must have hit her then, for I'd never seen the look of a woman who thought she'd lost so much as I did on Tally right then. I set down the coffee cup and was at the door in two long strides. If anyone else had any thought of what to say, they were holding it back; or maybe they were too shocked to believe what they were hearing. In a way I was a bit shocked myself at what I was saying, but I'd never been anything less than honest with those I knew, and when a man makes his decisions he sticks by them. And I reckon right then it was the feeling of loss in my own gut that hurt me more than any bruise I had on my body.

All of a sudden Tally was at my side, throwing her arms around my chest and just as suddenly letting go when I grimaced from the pain. She had that terrified look in her eyes as she spoke.

"Finn, I don't want anyone else!" She sounded as convincing as I'd ever heard her, with the same desperate need for me that I'd heard in her voice back in New Orleans when

I had left. "I only want you! Just you!!" Tears were forming in her eyes now, and her emotions were catching up with her thoughts.

"I felt that way once, too, Tally." Nothing had changed in my voice or the look on my face. It was hard and tough as any leather you'll ever see, but I knew that none of them had any idea how hard it was for me to do what I was doing. "I trusted you for four years without once seeing you, and I figured you did the same with me. But this ain't New Orleans, Tally, and it's no place for your kind of people. You may not believe it, Tally, but a man finds it hard enough to make a life out here without having to fight the people he's making the life for. And the way I figure it, when they don't want to share, when they don't want to trust, when they just want to own instead . . . well, then it ain't worth the making of it, that life.

"Seems to me you got a long way to go to learn about life out here."

"But Finn—"

By then I had finished what I had to say and was out the door. I didn't look back as I went to the corral and saddled a fresh horse. I heard her crying all the time, but I didn't look back.

I was suddenly aching all over and lonelier than I'd ever been before and the only time I looked back at her when I was leaving, Lisa was holding her in that doorway.

Pick Ax and Dean could help Tom with the runs. Me, I had other things to do.

Chapter 9

I wasn't certain just where I was going or what I would do, but seeing the way the fella who'd been spying on us had acted, well, hoss, people like that may get scared out of their skins, but I was willing to bet they were greedy as hell, too. As it turned out, I was right.

The trail he had taken was the same well-worn one Tom and I and near everyone else used to get to Sacramento, it being the biggest one in the area. And it didn't really surprise me that he headed that way, for I'd a suspicion that it was Johnstone's office he would wind up heading for. After all, a man ought to be paid for his work, such as it is.

He'd said that the man who had hired him was of medium to big build, which may have sounded pretty cut and dried, but it wasn't. You see, after you've been around a while you get to noticing certain things, and one of them is that not everyone sees the world or the people in it in the same light. My brother Nathan is big and bulky and, when pushed, can be meaner than any man I've ever seen. Me, I am somewhat skinnier than my brother but just as tall. I had another brother by the name of Sean. He is all of four years and it was from him I got some of that wisdom, for he was as curious as any tyke his age. Little Sean, he looked at all of us as just flat *big*. And Nathan, being the size he was, just sort of looked on the rest of the male population as small men, except for that Doniphan character and that's a whole 'nother canyon. Me, I'm tall and skinny so I gauge men by their bulk and height. And that's what got me to thinking the "boss" this fella had mentioned was likely Johnstone.

The man himself, the one we had caught, was tall and thicker than me, a bit like Tom Dobie, I reckon. So when he described the man who had hired him as medium to big in size, he might well have been talking about Johnstone, for the express agent was indeed a big man to tangle with. So I followed that fella's trail. Not too fast, you understand, for two cups of coffee was all I'd had, and it was hard enough to keep down the way my stomach was feeling. There didn't seem to be enough time to heal up all the pain I was feeling, but I was going to take as much as I could get. So I followed him slow, knowing I'd catch up with him in town.

If my body wasn't aching in one place, it was another, but all that pain didn't mean a thing next to what I was feeling on the inside, and I'm not talking about the coffee. I'd never felt as lonely as I did now, nor as unsure. Hell, I'd been through hard times before, but there was always a definite purpose to what had happened then. I'd been there at San Jacinto when my best friend, old Cooper Hansen, had died saving Nathan and Ellie, and I reckon that was one of the reasons I'd stayed out here, so I could somehow convince myself that what we had fought for was worth it. And ten years later I'd seen my Pa gunned down on the streets of Saint Louis. I had a purpose then, too, for it was nine months later that I caught up with the man who killed Pa and I buried him in the same hole he had me digging for my own grave. Strange thing was he was a friend I'd worked with one time, and I think it's the only time I ever enjoyed killing a person.

But now, well, now I wasn't sure about anything. I'd had a reason for going on after Cooper and Pa had died, for I had been close to them both and they had given me something to live for. Now I was leaving Tally, and it was as though I had never known her at all! With her it seemed as though one day she was everything in my life and the next day she was nothing, and I'll tell you, friend, that ain't nothing to base a marriage on. Maybe there was just one thing she could leave me, and it was the only thing I knew for sure. She had left me the loneliest man in the world and I didn't know what to do about it.

What had gotten into her? What had changed her so, or was I the one who had changed and didn't know it—or wouldn't admit it? How do you reach down inside yourself and give everything you've got for that one person who means so much to you, only to be treated as a scheming, conniving sort who was capable of nothing more than betrayal? I asked myself all of those questions over and over again as I followed that trail, and never once could I come up with an answer. Not even to the one question I couldn't escape asking: How do you go on when you've been hurt so badly that the scars will never heal and you'll never again give your love to another for fear of losing it? How?

I reckon if I'd been a drinking man like Tom Dobie, I'd have headed for the nearest saloon and drunk it dry to temporarily solve my problems, but after the previous night I wasn't about to try that. Besides, I picked up a certain amount of Irish practicality from Ma and right now it was telling me that Tally wasn't the only one to blame for what had happened. Someone had set me up with that woman in town who had caused all of the trouble, and if I couldn't have Tally, I could at least have the satisfaction of finding out who it was who had caused the trouble. And after I found them? Well, hoss, I'm a fairly law-abiding man, but right then I reckon what I had in mind for the culprit I was after was going to make those Blackfeet Sam'l Dean was talking about look tame! Real tame!

It was late afternoon when I got into town. The tracks I was following hadn't veered from the trail, so I'd been right in what I suspicioned about the man I was trailing. It was too bad that in all the excitement that afternoon none of us had taken the time to get his name. If I had it, I could have had Ray Wallace do some checking for me. As it was, I would have to do the tracking down my own self. But it would have to wait. The man would like as not still be around town when I came for him.

Some things change whether you want them to or not, and

I reckon your body is something that does just that. I had started out determined to find out what I could about this fella who'd been spying on us, and I would, by God, I would. But by the time I had neared town I wasn't sure how much more jostling around I could take without having someone look me over, so I headed for Timmley's office. He was one of the more reliable doctors in the area, a short, graying man who I couldn't remember ever seeing unshaven. He looked to be pushing fifty, but you never could tell out here, and as long as a man did his job proper there usually wasn't more than a handful who ever cared about age. That was one of the things I liked about this country.

"Well, now, Finn," he said stoically, looking me over as I grimaced entering his office, "seeing people with a look like that just makes me want to stop asking folks how they are when they come to me." I'd made enough people mad at me for one day, and I was needing his services, so I humored him some and tried smiling. "Need some fixing up, do you?"

"I didn't think I needed to ask," I said, slowly taking a seat by his operating table.

"You know, I sure am glad you boys have taken to them new-style shirts," he said as I unbuttoned my shirt. "Here, let me help you," he added from behind me and slowly pulled the shirt over my shoulders. When it was off he gave out a low whistle of what must have been astonishment. "Lordy, am I glad you're wearing them!" He was silent a moment before saying, "Finn, did you know that a good share of your left side is the goriest shade of reddish purple that I've ever seen?"

"Having that feeling was what brought me in, doc."

He did some poking around then and asked me how my insides were doing and how I came about it and all and I told him. And when he did that poking I knew what he meant about the new style of shirts that had become popular out here. They were called worsteds, made out of a combination of something and wool that did a bit better of taking the chill off the morning than buckskins ever did. Men like my brother who were set in their ways would be wearing buckskins 'til the last day they drew a breath. You could say it marked men like Nathan as the originals in this land, the ones who were the first. Me, I was there with Nathan when we came out to this frontier. But I was willing to accept some changes that my brother and his breed would never concede to. If they were smart, they'd realize that just like that worsted shirt there'd be more and different types to follow them. But right now the biggest difference between the shirt I had on and buckskins was that I'd have never been able to raise my arms as high as would be needed to get that buckskin over my head to take it off, I was that painful in the side.

"You fellas sure do live a rough life," he said, putting the final touches on my bandages. "All sorts of *accidents* happening." He said the word derisively as though he didn't quite believe what I had told him. "Fella come in yesterday needing a half dozen pieces of buckshot taken out of his leg. Damn fool was cleaning his shotgun! Can you believe it?"

"I reckon," I said automatically, for as important as a weapon was out here, there still seemed to be more than a casual number of men who got careless with "empty" guns. Then I went rigid in the back, the way you do when a muscle cramps up on you. Doc Timmley must have heard me groan, for he was soon back at my side.

"Anything wrong? Feeling more pain?" he asked with his usual concern.

"No, doc," I said. I wasn't about to tell him what it was that had surprised me, but I'm sure there was more than a little concern in my voice when I asked. "You recall who that fella was yesterday? The one who had buckshot in his leg?"

"No. Stranger to me. I just assume he was another one of those pilgrims struck with gold fever. Why?"

"Nothing, doc," I said, slowly putting my shirt on. "I thought I might have known him was all."

That wasn't quite the truth, but it wasn't a lie either, for one of those men who'd tried holding us up had taken some buckshot in the leg. They were masked and none of us got a clear look at those who had gotten away, but you can bet I'd know who it was when I came across him. Left handers weren't all that common, and unless this fella was some Daniel Boone from back east who fancied himself a two-gun man, well, the man who had taken the leg wound had a holster resting on his right hip, so I'd recognize him when I saw him again. I reckon that was one of the things you picked up out here right quick, having more active a mind than a mouth. A man had to be able to notice the little things, the details in life that could often be the difference between life and death. A bent twig in Indian country or, in this case, a man's shooting habits, could make all the difference in whether or not you made in through the day. The pilgrims, those easterners who came west and figured it for one big adventure or one big circus, would be the ones who looked for the obvious to guide them through life. But if there was one rule that was contrary to citified thinking, it was that the little things became the most important and perhaps the most obvious a man should look for. At least, if he was going to survive this land, and it was a land for survivors, indeed!

"Best thing you can do is get as much rest as you can, my boy," he said giving me a dose of something that was supposed to settle my stomach.

It was past suppertime when I left his office, but I didn't feel much like eating so I led my mount down to the livery. If I didn't have a place to rest tonight, at least my horse would. Herman worked the livery in town, or at least one of the better ones. Other than Flitsch he was the only other German that I knew all that well, a husky middle-aged man who was good at what he did and knew it. Tom and I had thrown some business his way once in a while, so after a bit of conversation while rubbing my mount down, I wangled him into letting me use the loft for the night. Not that I was cheap, you understand, but about then that hay seemed like the softest thing my body could stand for a decent night's rest.

Old Herman, he put faith in the people in Sacramento. He'd been there almost from the start and knew a good deal of the population, so he didn't put much of a guard on his stable when he left. But then, that was as it should be. If there was thievery and robbing going on, it was mostly out in the gold fields, although some of those who bought supplies would claim it was taking place here in town where the charges were exorbitant on some items. If nothing else, the talk of forming a vigilance committee that was going around was enough to put the fear of God in many a wayward man who might want to temporarily "borrow" a horse, for the rope he'd get for his trouble when he was caught was a permanent repayment that only came in one installment.

It was just after sundown when Herman left for the night, leaving the stable doors slightly ajar for anyone who might want to put his horse up before the night was through. I took pains in slowly climbing the ladder to the second story loft and finding a suitable chunk of hay to lay my weary body on.

My body wanted to sleep, but there was planning I had to do yet, so I forced myself to stay awake. I had to figure out what exactly I was going to do about the man I had trailed. My hunch was that he was working for Johnstone of Adams Express, but I couldn't prove it. If I were to hobble into Johnstone's office and confront the man with the charge, he'd laugh at me, of that I was sure. Still, there had to be a way.

Then my thoughts shifted to Tally and what I had said to her and how strong a statement I'd really made. It was the truth, all right, but as harshly as I'd said it, she undoubtedly had taken it for revenge for her own actions. I had told her to leave, that she didn't belong in this country, and when I returned she would be gone. Hell, right then I didn't feel like going back at all! I reckon it was a mixture of pride and guilt that made me feel that way. I wasn't even sure that I wanted to carry on the freighting trade with Tom. Maybe it was time to move on, to find another part of the land that hadn't been seen yet. Maybe Nathan was right about having too many people around. They could crowd you all right, and be as bothersome as hell sometimes. But to tell the truth, I had something inside me that was pulling me both ways at the same time. One voice said to leave, hit the trail, and find a new life. Things weren't working out, and there was always some other hill to head for, like that old bear. And the other voice was saying that I still loved her, still needed Tally. I'll tell you, hoss, I'd have rather fought the whole Comanche nation than be responsible for making a decision like that. But if I didn't want to make the choice, I at least didn't have to think about it any more, for my thoughts were interrupted by the slow creak of the stable door as two men stepped inside.

" 'Bout time you got here," one said as the second joined him. It was dark now and all I could see were shadows from the dimly lit street lamps of the town, but I was a curious sort anyway, so I rolled over on my stomach as easy as I could without making any noticeable noises and cocked an ear toward the conversation.

"Jory says they were raising hell with one another out there today, just like the boss planned it." One of them lit a cigarette he'd been rolling, and I thought I saw him raise his eyebrows as the match flared. Then both were speaking in hushed whispers, and I felt a chill going down my spine. I was so engrossed in them that I had forgotten about me. I had been so curious about what they were saying that when I'd rolled over I'd forgotten to pull out my own pistol! If I'd made enough of a noise to get their attention, I was gone beaver! A lot of good the Colt's was gonna do me now, as I was laying on it. I reckon it was one of those times you remember what little religion you do have, for it's then, when a man's in a tight spot, that he calls on his Maker for some guidance. Not that I couldn't take care of myself, you understand. It's just that a body feels a mite more secure if the Almighty sees fit to let him keep his body for just a tad more time before turning the spirit loose. And I reckon He was watching over the fool in me for playing as dangerous a game as I was, for the only sounds those two noticed came from some of the horses stabled below.

"You tell Bill I got the gang set for another holdup in a few days. First, there's some business he wants took care of," one of them said before parting. His cohort acknowledged him, and the two turned to go, leaving the stable door open a few feet. And when they did I saw them through the faint light of the street. I didn't recognize the voices of either of them, but I knew who one of them was now.

He was the fella who walked away favoring his right leg.

Chapter 10

As much as I had on my mind I didn't think I'd be able to sleep at all that night, for the parts of their conversation I had caught were beginning to explain some of the things that had been happening. But there are times that exhaustion is hard to fight and that night was one of them, for one minute I was thinking about what those characters had said and the next I heard the stable door creaking open.

"You get enough sleep, Finn?" I heard Herman's voice boom as the door continued to creak and daybreak showed through.

"Yeah, Herman, sure," I mumbled, knowing that I'd not feel worth much until I at least had my coffee.

I was awfully sore getting up, but from some of those medical books Lisa had that I'd dipped into, well, that was some sort of a sign that I was healing. Not that a body could ever tell it by the ache in the bones. But I took heart anyway. I was slow climbing down that ladder, but noticed that apparently the concoction the doctor had given me had taken hold, for my stomach was growling and I had a ravenous feeling in me that told me I hadn't eaten for near a week, although two days was more like it.

"You vant da hoss now?" He knew how to start the day right, Herman did. The man really had to be in a bad mood not to try to make the rest of the world feel good too. And times like this, well, hoss, it was nice having people like Herman around, for his attitude seemed almost contagious.

"Not just yet, Herman. I think I'll get me a bite to eat and maybe be back later in the morning for him."

"Ya," he said, still smiling, "any time."

The more expensive-type restaurants wouldn't open until later when the "respectable" clientele, they being the rich ones, would be ready to dine. But thank God not everyone had struck it rich, for there were still those of us who got up before light and wanted to get done as much as we could. And there were other eateries that knew it, too, some staying open all night and working as much of a swing shift at cooking as those in the mines did earning the dust to pay for it. I found one that wasn't too far off and had an empty table in the corner. Actually, it was some rather crude wood that had been cut and hammered enough to fit two bodies and their meals to it, three if you could find a skinny man like Pick Ax to fit between the wall and the table. That may sound a bit eerie to you, but this proprietor was making sure that the only thing that left his eatery was the food he was serving and the customers who ate it. The wooden table had been built into the floor and was immobile at best.

I was about to order ham and eggs when the fella running the operation came over and set a plate before me. It was beefsteak and fried spuds, and they were as big and ugly as this fella was. I got the notion he figured I'd approve of whatever he put down in front of me.

"I'll bring some coffee." It was a statement more than a request, but what could you expect from someone who had the face of a stoic Ute? Besides, my stomach wasn't any too particular at what I attacked to feed it, so long as it wasn't buffalo chips or cow pie. So I did just that, attacked the food. I was used to eating my beefsteak well done, but this fella must have had more customers than he had time to cook for because the meat was a bit rare in the center. The only thing that saved the taste was the burnt-to-a-crisp outside of the beef. But I had things to do, and not being fed just the right food for a day's start was the last thing I intended to lodge as far as a complaint that day.

As I ate I tried to piece together what I had heard the night before and what had been happening. There was no doubt that the man leaving that livery had been the one who had visited Doc Timmley as well as the one who'd taken some lead trying to hold us up. Favoring his right leg like he did might be circumstantial to Ray Wallace, but the man also had a piece of cowhide bulging from that right hip and I was betting that if I got close in a good light I'd find some blood on it if it was the same holster he'd worn during the hold up.

Another piece of coincidence was the remark about someone raising hell, "just like the boss planned it," as the man had said. It could be anywhere or anybody they were talking about, but I was just too tired of strange things happening to me to believe otherwise. From what he had said, the whole thing had been as engineered as an explosive charge set in one of those mines that was being worked. Having that knowledge gave me some mixed emotions too. At first I was glad that I could take some evidence to Tally to prove to her that I hadn't been trailing another woman. But following that was a feeling of anger that such a plan had succeeded in tearing me and the woman I loved apart! It made me so damn mad that I near bent the fork in my hand in half.

And then there was the reference to Bill the two had made. Who was he? From the way they were talking, he could well have been behind the trouble with Tally as well as the holdup. But who was he? My first instinct had been to go after Johnstone, he being the braggart that he was, but I began to wonder if it could be him after all. His name was Hiram as I recalled, or at least that was how Tom had introduced him that day. Still, it was worth checking out. I figured Johnstone was simply too cocky, too self-assured about talking over our outfit, not to be tied in with this mess somehow.

When I finished, I headed for Ray Wallace and the sheriff's office. One way or another he would get involved with what I was doing, especially if it concerned the rash of robberies that had taken place of late. One of the men had mentioned a Jory, who must have been the man I had caught at our place and trailed into town the day before. Being a lawman, you get to noticing a good share of your citizenry and what their habits are so you can gauge their actions and reactions when the case arises. And like I said, Ray Wallace was one of the best lawmen I'd ever seen.

"Yeah, I've heard of a Jory," Ray said. "Works with the horses out at the corrals that the Adams Express runs. Why? You having trouble with him?"

"That's a fact. I caught him out at the cabin yesterday doing some kind of spying on us. I told him to git if he valued his life, but he wound up coming back here."

"I wouldn't stake my job on whether my authority stretches out to your place," Ray said, reaching for his pistol and holstering it, "but if you've got something that could tie into these gangs operating the area, I'll just tag along."

"I appreciate it, Ray."

I had planned on going it alone, but having the law with you can come in handy at times, and the truth was I wasn't too awful anxious to tangle with Johnstone again. With the sheriff along I might be able to get some answers to a few other questions I hadn't told Ray about. Like who was Bill?

The Adams Express Company ran a two-story building of its own. The company itself had first been established in San Francisco in 1849 when its founder, Alvin Adams, had the foresight to see just how much money an express business could reap in a gold rush such as this. I'd been to Frisco and seen the three-story building which housed the express company there where it had taken to opening up a bank as well. In doing so the Adams Express Company had won a reputation as one of the leading corporations in California. It's headquarters were in San Francisco, as was a new company operated by a Wells and Fargo partnership. But for my money it was Sacramento that was the hub of the transportation of this territory. True, nearly all of the ore we carried into town wound up going to San Francisco, but you had to consider that many a time the total for one day's worth of gold taken from here to Frisco was in excess of a million dollars. But comparing express companies and their territories wasn't all I had on my mind as Ray and I entered the Adams building.

The inner office was what you'd expect, a lot of clerks doing the rushing around while the bosses did the decision making. I got the impression that they'd not had much cause to see the law enter their office, though, for things sort of got quiet as Ray and I entered. Or maybe Johnstone had given everyone my description and told them to be on the lookout for me.

"Don't let me disturb you, folks," Ray said in a voice that was no louder than normal but let them all know he wanted every one of them to acknowledge his presence. It was his show, so I let him look the place over until he found Johnstone's desk, an area that had been my first discovery. "You got a few minutes?" he said, approaching Johnstone. Once again he was letting it be known that he was going to have his few minutes whether the express agent had them to spare or not.

"Of course," Johnstone said, offering a seat. For a big man he obviously wasn't used to being treated this way, and the effort at being hospitable was putting a strain on him.

"No thanks," Ray said, "we likely won't be here too long."

"Whatever you say, sheriff."

"Mr. Johnstone, I'll get right to the point. Callahan here says one of your hands was out to his place yesterday. Says he caught him spying on him. Jory is his monicker, I believe. Do you care to tell me what you know about that?" Ray folded his arms when he was through, as though he was prepared to stand there 'til hell froze over or he got his answers. It crossed my mind that his stance together with that plug ugly face on the cook I'd seen earlier would make a perfect statue of a wooden Indian.

"Well, now, sheriff, those could be pretty serious charges."

"Ain't nobody gonna find out how serious they are until they're proved, Johnstone," I said feeling a bit cocky, "and I got a feeling they'll prove out as sure as a bear takes to hibernating."

"I have cause not to like you, Callahan," Johnstone said,

"but I'll ignore your remarks and just tell the sheriff that he keeps lousy company."

"You're getting off the subject, Mr. Johnstone," Ray said, raising an eyebrow.

"Jory's out back at the corrals," the man said. "Why don't we go ask him? I certainly don't know what you're talking about." He picked up his hat and was halfway to the back door with Ray before I moved.

"Tell me something, friend," I said loud enough to stop both men in their tracks. A befuddled look came to Johnstone's face as I glanced down at the nameplate perched on his desk. HIRAM W. JOHNSTONE was what it read. "What's your middle name?"

I had Ray puzzled now too, but it was the bigger man who got a sudden look of worry on his face. "Well, uh, uh, it's Wallace, yes, that's it." For a simple answer to a simple question, he sure was sounding awful nervous. That was giving me an idea that seemed more and more to be proving out. And the idea was that Johnstone was the head of that gang. Sure, Wallace could be his middle name, but the way he was acting it could just as surely be William, too. And William was Bill. It was all circumstantial evidence, of course, but it all fit in very nicely.

Jory was the man I had figured him to be. But he turned almighty pale in the face when he saw me coming. This was one man who had no fear of the law right then, for I had told him I'd do him in the next time I saw him. Fact is, he was looking as though all he'd need was his Sunday-go-to-meeting suit and the undertaker's pine box to be ready for his Maker.

"Jory, the sheriff tells me that you don't spend your time just working for me." Johnstone sounded a bit embarrassed at not knowing what his employees were up to and it sounded awful real, but I wasn't setting it down in stone, you can believe that. "You do a little . . . side work other than your job here at Adams?"

The wrangler shrugged. "Man's gotta make a living best he knows how."

"What you were doing yesterday wasn't too healthy,

friend,'' I said, hard enough so he would know he wasn't a *friend* of mine.

"Is that right, son?'' Ray asked. "Were you out to the Callahan place yesterday?''

"Well, what if I was?'' A new defiance had come to the man now, but I reckon it was to be expected. Most men who have their back to the wall will put up as false a front as any saloon unless their real bravado shows up first. And I didn't take this fella for being any too brave. Not a'tall.

"Well, now, Jory, I'll tell you,'' the sheriff said, a frown coming to his face. "The folks in this town don't mind people being neighborly with 'em, although some of the ladies say that once in a while some fella will try catching a look-see through their window whilst they're in their under-things.'' Here he paused as his face got harder. "But any man who takes to *spying* on a man and his family and gets *paid* for it, well, son, there's gotta be something on the books that says it ain't lawful. And if there ain't, I'm gonna have you setting in my hoosegow for as long as it takes me to get hold of Henry Clay and Dan'l Webster back east to find out for sure.''

"You know those two gentlemen?'' Johnstone asked, apparently impressed.

"Surprised you, did it?'' It had not only surprised the express agent, but me as well. Ray could tell a story or two when he wanted to, but for the most part he was pretty close-mouthed about his past. A lot of men were like that, usually because they either wanted to forget the past and start over, or had learned long ago that getting a big head only leads to a big mouth and that, my friend, is one hell of a way to lose your teeth. "Yes, I know them,'' he went on. "They've each got twenty and some years on me, but I got quite an education from them in my youth, before any of us ever got to being recognized as more'n we were.''

"In that case, sheriff, I feel honored,'' Johnstone said. Like a lot of businessmen I'd seen, he tended to spread it on right thick when he thought it would give him an in to some new area. I reckon that was one reason I never cared for politics; I never could stand someone giving me a pat on the back and a kick in the ass at the same time. And Ray wasn't having any of it either.

"Don't feel honored, Mr. Johnstone," Ray said with disgust. "Just feel like you're less one employee." Then, turning his gaze to the wrangler, he said, "Jory, you're going with me. Finn, keep an eye on him while Mr. Johnstone fills out some papers inside for me." As the two left I heard Ray say, "Mr. Johnstone, I want to talk to you about some stagecoach robberies that I've got a lead on. . . ."

I never was sure if it was the sheriff's leaving me alone there with this Jory fella or the words he spoke as he walked off concerning the holdups that had been going on, but one of the two gave this wrangler the same scared look he'd had on his face the day before when Sam'l Dean had told his Blackfoot war story.

Nor was I aware of any papers that had to be signed by the lawman when he was taking a man in; that sort of thing usually came later. So all I could figure was that Ray was leaving this bird with me to see what I could get out of him. One way or another something had put the fear of God in this man, and that's usually a good time to pour a few more coals on the fire . . . just before you tell a man he's going to have to walk on them if he's at all concerned with saving his skin.

"I heard a couple of men down by the livery last night, friend, and they got to talking about a holdup and being out to my place." That wasn't quite the truth, but as scared as he was, I figured throwing in my own hunches was as good as anything else right then. "One of them even mentioned your name. That's how I tracked you down, you know." I must have sounded like I knew every last detail about his life, for there was a line of sweat forming atop his upper lip and forehead. "They mentioned a fella named Bill. Is he your boss? Was he the one sent you out to my place?" I waited for a response, and by the looks of him, he was weighing the alternatives and what would happen to him with each one. And I had a notion he didn't figure he'd come out much more than at the bottom of the dung heap either way. "You let us know if that Bill's a part of these holdups been going on and the sheriff might take it into consideration when your time comes," I went on.

"He's just the sheriff, Callahan, what good's he gonna do me?"

"Oh, I don't know," I said with a shrug, "a man who hobnobs with the likes of Webster and Clay, I'd figure he likely knows a few lawyers and judges to boot." I had no idea if that was the case with Ray Wallace, but it wouldn't surprise me at all if he did have a few connections he hadn't told anyone about.

"You sure?" He was thinking on it now and giving more serious thought, if the sound of his voice was any indication.

"Friend, the only thing I ever guaranteed was that the sun comes up in the east and sets in the west most days. But you tell Ray Wallace what you know about all this and . . . well, I may even forget about taking you back out to my place and letting Sam'l Dean stake you out like he was figuring."

He had a worried look about him now, the look of a man who's bought the farm no matter which way he jumps. He was in trouble now with the law, but if he helped the sheriff, he'd be in trouble with whoever it was he had been working for. Sort of like picking the lesser of two evils, as the fella said.

"What I want to know is, who is Bill?" I said. "You said you'd never seen him before. It wouldn't be Johnstone in there, would it?" I added, throwing a thumb over my shoulder.

He never had a chance to answer, for it was then that two shots rang out. They came from my rear, both at the same time, one of them slamming into Jory's chest, throwing him back into a corral post. He had the damnedest look of surprise on his face then, as though the blow against his back from the corral had sent a shock through his body. Either that or he had recognized the man who had shot him, never figuring him for doing such a thing! The second shot took the hat off my head and I found myself crawling for cover as I dove to the ground and pulled my Colt's out.

It was all over by the time I could get my bearings, the

only movement coming from my left as Ray and Johnstone came rushing toward me. Both had guns drawn, both looking to each side as they ran, as puzzled as I was at what had happened.

"You all right, Finn?" Ray asked, still looking about. The only thing holding Jory up was an arm draped over the corral post as a large pool of blood spread about his shirt front and his head sagged to the side, lifeless.

"I reckon," I said, picking up my hat with my free hand. "But I'll tell you, hoss, that's a helluva way to get gray hair."

"Know what you mean," Ray said as he holstered his pistol and began to inspect Jory. "Only an army rifle or one of them Hawkens could do this much damage. Must have been a distance shot."

"Yes," Johnstone said. "Over there, see," he added, pointing to a cloud of dust to the south. I was certain I'd seen the agent glance in that direction as soon as he came into sight. There was something about the man I just didn't feel was right.

"That must be him."

"Them," I corrected. I said it hard, looking Johnstone straight in the eye as I did, thinking he'd made the mistake deliberately. "There was *two* shots fired at once and I ain't seen the men yet could shoot a rifle from each shoulder at the same time. Especially those bigger cannons."

By now a crowd had gathered, many of them workers with the stock. Johnstone, ever the businessman, was about to shoo them all back to work when Ray grabbed two men to take care of Jory's body.

"Just hold on a minute, Johnstone," he said, looking out over the crowd. Then he said, "You people have been complaining about these stage holdups of late. Well, now's your chance to get something done about 'em. I'm needing a few men to ride with me after a couple of them, and I mean right now. I'm sure Mr. Johnstone won't mind a few of his own men volunteering for that." He gave a side glance at the agent now standing beside him, and somehow I got the idea he was testing him.

"Of course not," Johnstone said a bit reluctantly. "You heard the sheriff, saddle up."

"You coming along, Finn?"

"Not this time, Ray." I looked down at the blood-smeared body of the wrangler. "I've got a feeling I'm gonna have enough trouble out at my own place."

"Good enough. Check in with me if you need any help. He turned to Johnstone. "What about you?" I could tell Ray was getting as suspicious as I was about the man but knew he would only operate within the limits of the law.

"No," Johnstone replied, more nervous than I'd seen him before. "I think not, sheriff. I've a business to run, you know." With that he left before either Ray or I could say anything else. "Real public-spirited, ain't he?" Ray said to me as he watched the man leave.

"Yeah," I said, but that wasn't all I was thinking, not by a long shot.

I had gotten out to the main street again when I met Tom and Sam'l Dean heading my way, both perched on the wagon.

"What happened?" Tom asked.

"Turn this thing around and get it back to the livery. We're gonna need horses for what I've got in mind," I told them.

"Again?" Sam'l Dean sounded as cynical as ever. "Boy, do you know you're gonna wear out that livery man's faith in you?"

"How's that?" I said climbing onto the back of the wagon.

"Well, you're damn sure wearing out his horses."

I explained what had happened and what I had learned as Tom got the rig headed for the other side of town. And the more I explained the faster he got the wagon going. By the time we got there, the two had heard it all. Herman said he'd take care of the wagon and its team and loaned out three good mounts to us. I had a blue roan, one of those mahogany bays that'll run their hearts out for you if need be, and I'd a hunch that was going to be the case.

"So you think these backshooters are part of the holdup gang?" Dean asked mounting up. Tom and I swung up in the saddle then, and I could see by the expression on his face that such movements were reminding him of how weary his body was, just as much as my own.

"Right now I don't care about the holdups," I said, feeling the mad grow in me again. "I'm just tired of being shot at and pushed around in general."

"It does get tiresome," Tom said.

We lit out like there was a fire chasing us. I don't know about Dean, but I knew the fire was building inside Tom as much as it was me then, as much as was the hurt and mad. Tom was going back because Lisa was there, and Sam'l Dean was likely tagging along because, as much as he hated to admit it, he enjoyed the excitement of what was happening. The man simply didn't show it as much as his cohort, Pick Ax. Me, I could say I was heading back for Tally, but I wasn't. I would have liked to have been able to say it, but it wouldn't have been true. The truth was just what I had said. I was tired of being pushed around and shot at. What I found myself particularly mindful of was the fact that Johnstone had stayed behind while Ray and his volunteers went after the assassins, leaving him free to do as he wished. Then there was the other man I had seen in the shadows the night before, and the fact that I couldn't account for his whereabouts made me that much madder.

And then, I hadn't asked Tom why he and Sam'l were in town. We didn't have an ore shipment that day that I recalled, so it was likely they had brought Tally in to town to catch a stage back east. So it didn't matter what I thought about the woman; she was out of my life now. The strange thing was I was feeling lonesome right then. But I reckon it takes a while to get over a person like that.

To put her out of my mind, I tried to concentrate on what had been going on in the past few days that had so turned my life upside down. If I didn't know better, I would have thought that I had been jinxed by the woman in my life, for it seemed that everything had been happening to me, to us, since right before she had arrived.

First there was the sabotaging of our equipment, after Johnstone all but swore he'd take our company from us. Perhaps it was only from my point of view that he seemed a man on the shady side of the law, but then not much had looked the way it should have of late.

Then there were the attempted holdups, two in one week. Was it fate? Simply our turn to be held up by these ruthless highwaymen? Or was it more than that? Again it seemed as though I was jinxed in the matter, as though an aura of bad luck had been cast on me with Tally's arrival. True, it could have been coincidence, but thinking on it gave me the notion that it wasn't. I became particularly mindful of that split-second during the second holdup when I had that feeling pass through me that I'd seen one of the men before. Just thinking about it sent a chill down my spine.

And a funny thing happened just then. I was suddenly able to recall the incident two nights ago when Tom and I had been soundly beaten in the alley in town. It gave me an eerie feeling, for up until then I'd not been able to recall anything that had happened that night, after Tom and I had started drinking. At least nothing after having our supper meal. Now I recalled the net being thrown over me very well!

But I had little more time to think about it, for it was then that we topped the rise above our cabin.

Chapter 11

Whoever it was down there hadn't seen us, not yet.

There were a half dozen riders a hundred yards off, leaving the area as fast as they could. Another four or five were in front of the cabin, two of them dismounted. The horsemen sat their saddles as dutifully as any guard, rifles nestled in the crooks of their arms. The two on the ground were husky from what I could see, but then we were some fifty yards off. I took all of this in at a glance, but it wasn't that so much as the sight of Lisa standing in front of the men that got my attention. And Tom's. One of them had grabbed her by the wrist and was pulling her toward him.

"No!" she screamed. "You can't make me go! I won't!!''

By that time Tom and I had drawn our Dragoons. And I reckon that was when hell took a holiday you might say, for one helluva lot began to happen as the three of us put the heels to our mounts.

Sam'l Dean put the reins in what was left of his teeth and charged off at a half left angle at the three mounted men. He brought his Colt's revolving shotgun to his shoulder then and let fly a load about halfway there, getting the attention of all three horsemen as he cocked and fired again.

At the same time as Tom and I made our descent on the cabin, out staggered Pick Ax, bandaged up and all.

"Let go of her!" he yelled in that frail voice of his.

But they would have none of it; one of the men on foot brought up his pistol and shot point blank at the old-timer. Pick Ax went reeling back up against the wall, but he wasn't through yet. All the while he had been bringing up a pistol of his own and when I heard the ear-shattering boom I knew it was the Walker Colt he had taken from the wall. There was no mistaking what gun it was as his shot hit its mark and the man who had shot him was physically picked up off the ground and sent sailing backward a good six feet before landing on his own back, dead.

Both Tom and I were nearing the cabin then, and Lisa wisely stepped out of range as I brought my Dragoon up and snapped off a shot at the man who had let her go and now drawn his pistol. I hit him in the shoulder, knocking him back, but it was Tom's deadly aim that killed him as his own shot landed dead center in the man's chest.

We were off our horses in an instant as Lisa ran to Pick Ax, who had slumped down against the wall in a sitting position. There was no question that he was dying as we approached. A look over my shoulder and I saw Dean riding toward us, two of the mounted men gone while the third horse strayed in the field.

"Let me get—" Lisa started to say but stopped when Pick Ax grabbed her sleeve.

"No." He spoke softly now, softer than before as the energy seemed to drain from his body. Seeing him like that, with blood all over his chest reminded me of my old friend Cooper Hansen at San Jacinto so long ago. I couldn't help but wonder then if, when a man comes to his end, he doesn't find that there is so much to say but so little time to do it in. I had felt that way when Cooper died and had the same feeling now.

"We're even now," he said to Lisa. "I saved your life."

"Yes," I heard her say just as softly, tears running down her cheeks as she tried to look grateful, though she must have been feeling like hell. "Yes, you saved my life."

Tom silently took Lisa in his arms as she wept, and Pick Ax slowly turned his head to me, coughing.

"You find that girl and keep her, boy." For an instant I

thought I saw a touch of remorse in his face as he spoke. "She ain't a quitter, just misguided."

"You never could shoot," Sam'l Dean said, a hitch in his voice as well.

"Uglier than sin, too," he said with a smile, now looking at Dean, perhaps the one true friend he had ever had in the world. Then his head slumped to his side.

"Maybe, old-timer," I said passing a hand over his eyes, "but you ain't no quitter either."

Tom took Lisa inside as Dean leaned his shotgun against a piece of wood. If anyone had lost someone right then, it was he. I knew he had seen Pick Ax come charging out of the cabin the same as Tom and I had, and it was then I thought I saw a change in him as he rode hell-for-leather toward the three armed men while Tom and I headed for the cabin. And what little I'd seen of him then reminded me of a reckless young lad trying to prove himself to the pack he was running with. Of course, it was the same kind of riding and shooting and bravado you could find on the plains down in Texas by any man who called himself a Ranger. I knew that for a fact because I'd been one.

"I'll get the shovel," he said in a sad voice.

I kept my own gun out as I headed for the field to inspect the man Dean had shot.

"He's dead," I heard the old man say as he saw me walking out in that direction. The sadness had turned to hate now, and I knew that the fire was building in him too. It was just a damn shame that a man had to lose a friend as close as he and Pick Ax had been to get that fired up.

When I got to the man I knew instantly that Dean was right. He had caught a full load in the chest at close range. I hadn't noticed it at first, but apparently the three horsemen had had masks on, for what reason I didn't know. But looking down at the man, the mask still covering his face, I had that strange feeling again, a chill running down my back. Damn but it was scary! Then I recognized him as the man I had seen that day of the holdup. The one I'd stared at for that one split-second that gave me the strangest shudder to my insides. As I gathered up his rifle and pistol and went through his pockets for any extra shot and ball he might have, I had that same, uncontrollable shiver, as though my subconscious was trying to tell me something and I couldn't figure out what it was.

After I collected the guns and ammunition from the other two outlaws, both of them strangers to me, I set it all on the porch and headed for the barn to get a shovel and give Dean a hand. But when I walked over to where the old-timer had started to dig he only waved me away.

"If you don't mind, son, this is one grave I'll dig by myself."

"Sure, Sam'l. I understand."

"Why don't you go on back to the others." He stopped digging, glanced around at the three bodies of the outlaws on the ground. "These birds ain't in no hurry," he said with a bitterness I'd not heard in him before. "Only thing waiting for them is a one-way ticket to hell and a lifetime of being burned."

One of the outlaws must have gotten off a shot in our direction, for Tom was being treated for a flesh wound to his left shoulder when I entered the cabin.

"What happened?" I asked Lisa as she patched up her husband.

"They rode up about an hour ago. At first I thought they wanted water or directions, but they were down and off their horses before I could get back in the cabin. We were gonna fight 'em off, and I guess they thought Pick Ax was too sick to handle a gun, but—"

"Wait a minute," I said. "We? You said *we*?"

"Yes. Tally and I. Why do you—"

"But, what were you doing in town?" I asked Tom. "Didn't you bring Tally in to get a stage back east?"

"Tally? No." He frowned, dismissing the thought. "Old Man Nellor came by after you left yesterday afternoon, asking if I'd make a special trip for him today. Seems he had more dug out and ready to go than he thought. Hell, Finn, that's what me and Dean had just finished when we met you this morning."

"She stayed?" I must have sounded as stunned as I felt.

"After what I said she stayed?" I was beginning to feel like a fool after all of the thoughts I'd been thinking about her.

"You know, Finn," Lisa said, tying off one of the bandages on Tom, "he was right."

My mind was so full of trying to figure out why she had stayed that at first I didn't hear her.

"Who?"

"Pick Ax."

"Oh."

"Tally and I had a long talk after you left, Finn."

"That's right, hoss. They kicked me and Dean out of the place for a couple hours, damn near 'til sunset!"

"I guess Pick Ax overheard a lot of it," she continued. "Not that it's worth anything, but if you want my opinion, I think both of you were expecting too much from each other when you met this time." She set down her medicinals, placed an understanding hand on mine. The eyes I looked into now were those of a woman who understood all too well the feelings of another woman in love. "You've both forgotten that it's been four years since you've seen one another and that people change." Tom had a curious look to his face now, as though he suspected that his wife was romancing me now instead of him. But I knew better than that, could sense in Lisa's voice and manners that she now wanted everything between Tally and me to be as it should as much as I once did. The trouble was that I was no longer sure.

"You poor man," she said, a sad sort of smile coming to her face as she spoke, almost as I remembered Ma talking to me as a youngster. "People change, Finn. You can read Will Shakespeare and Cooper and Byron until the end of time and the words will never change, will they?"

"No." She had me confused, and I wasn't all that sure I knew what she was getting at.

"To hear you talk, you've gone from a fourteen-year-old greenhorn down in Texas to a man of the world out here who runs a freighting business. You've been a lot of places and seen a lot of people and done a lot of things. I know, Finn, for I was with you on one of those expeditions. A lot of time has gone by and you've seen a lot of the people and a good share of this land change. Isn't that so?''

"Yeah, but so what?" I was still confused.

"You just don't see, do you?"

"No. No, I don't."

"Finn, when two people are in love with each other as much as you and Tally are, well, I guess they only see the change in the one they love . . . not in themselves."

"But I haven't changed," I said, sure that she was wrong. "Tally's the one who's changed, not me."

"That's the same thing she said about you when we talked." The smile was gone from her face now as a soft, serious sort of look took its place. I'd seen it before on her and knew it. It was the kind of look she took on when she wanted to make a point but didn't want to scare you off. Not just then, anyway. "Tally told me she could only remember the good times she'd had with you in New Orleans. The time she spent with a soft, gentle man who made her quite happy in a number of ways." The smile returned for an instant as she blushed.

"Yes," I said, drawing on my memory and recalling those two weeks we shared together. "Yeah, I remember her that way, too. Easy to talk to and understanding. Not like she's been since she's arrived here. She's nothing like that now." I must have sounded fairly stubborn then, for in the back of my mind I was determined to prove myself right.

"Finn," she said, raising her eyebrows, "you're not that way either."

"Huh?" I squinted at her, flabbergasted at the improbability of what she had said. Then, turning to my partner I said, "Tom, have I changed? Do you think I've changed?" But I could see that Tom didn't want to take any side on this argument lest he lose, and lose he would.

"Beats the hell outta me," he said, rising and putting his hat on. "I'm just a married man trying to make a living. Now, if you'll excuse me, I think I'll get Sam'l a cup of coffee and tend to the one thing I do know. Horses." He gave us both a scant look of derision, as though he were glad to be getting back to a job where the only fool he had to worry about was the one who argued with a mule. But then, Tom always had made it clear that he preferred animals to humans, particularly since the animals seldom argued with him.

"Yes, you have changed, Finn," Lisa said when Tom had gone. "You've taken on the responsibilities of a business with Tom, and like it or not that's made you a harder man. Especially when you start giving orders and making ultimatums like you did yesterday to Tally. You didn't give her half a chance."

"But, Lisa, she didn't give *me* half a chance, either!"

"Yes," she said, a disheartening look coming to her face. "Yes, there's that." It was a weak point in her argument, and I knew she didn't want to admit it, even if it was true. She walked to the stove then, and I wasn't sure whether or not she was going to cry as she poured a cup of coffee. It sure seemed like she wanted to, and if it would have done any good, I believe she might have. But I knew her to be a strong woman, drawing much of her strength from Tom over the years, and she wouldn't cry.

She set the cup down in front of me and took a seat across from me at the table. Then she took hold of my hand and squeezed it gently. I had a feeling that what she was about to say would pain her, for when she spoke it was with a desperateness I'd not heard in her before. "I do know this, Finn. That woman loves you more than you have a right to know. Maybe I sense it because she reminds me so much of how I felt about Tom when I first met him. She's as confused about what to do as you are, Finn, but don't doubt for a moment that she loves you or that she'd do anything for you. You just have to give each other a chance.

"Tom and I have been together four years now, Finn, and I don't regret any of them. We've grown together and we fight, but . . . we've made up, too. If you and Tally would give each other a chance, I think you'd find out that you're both so right for each other."

She was silent then, and I swear I've never seen a more pleading look of hopefulness in a woman's eyes in my life. And maybe she was right. Maybe everything had started off all wrong, what with the theft of Tally's luggage and the sabotaging of our rig and the holdups . . . and the woman. Tally hadn't been here a week, and I'd had more excitement in my life in one form or another than since I'd first met her back during the Mexican War. I had been pretty rough on her the day before, just as Lisa had said. I had—

"Lisa," I said, now grabbing out and catching her by the wrist as I felt a desperation of my own come on. "You said 'we,' Lisa. You said 'we.' " I quickly took in the cabin, realizing that in all of the talk I had forgotten about Tally's own presence. "Where is she?"

A look of shame came over her and she paled in the face.

"I did it for her," she said, pleadingly. Her strength was gone now.

"Did what?" I had that fire building in me again as the anger grew.

"The men who left as you were coming down the rise."

"Yes."

"They had her," she said, a tear rolling down her cheek.

"Damn!" I pounded a fist into the table, not even feeling the pain that shuddered through my side.

"They said if I didn't stall you for half an hour, they'd kill her!!"

Chapter 12

I spilled the coffee pushing myself away from the table. I must have had a killing look about me, for Lisa had fear in her eyes. But in that second or two it took me to get up, well, hell, I don't know what happened to my mind, but I knew that what Lisa had said about Tally and me wasn't simply to stall me from going after her. It was the truth. Like it or not it needed to be told, and for all the excitement that had been happening, well I reckon it got said at the right time. I knew then that whatever it was I'd been telling myself or everyone else, it was for Tally I had come riding hell-for-leather back to this place.

I kissed Lisa on the forehead and gave her a wink as I tried to force a smile. "Tom's got one helluva woman."

"Tom!" I yelled, stepping outside the cabin door. When the big man appeared in the barnyard, I said, "Saddle up two horses. We got places to go."

"Make it three." The words came from Sam'l Dean who stood waist deep in the hole he was digging. When both Tom and I gave a strange look at him, he seemed to get all sorts of blustery. "Listen," he said, waving a finger at Tom, then me, "you pups are gonna be going up against some tough odds if them six I seen riding off'n here was any indication. So you're gonna need a good man riding shotgun for ya."

"And you're it," Tom said, knowing it was a wasted question.

"You betcher . . . bottom dollar," Dean said, noticing Lisa before he finished the sentence. Still he had conviction in it no matter what the words were and I knew there'd be three of us.

"Tom," Lisa sang out, "make it four mounts."

"And where do you think you're going?" I asked with a frown.

But she, too, was determined to go, planting her hands on her hips as she spoke to me, just like some boss talking to his employee. "For the last few days, every time you two have gone off and come back you've been in trouble and the worse for wear. Now, if you think I'm waiting for you three to come back half dead another time after traipsing all over hell's creation, well, you'd better think again."

I held up four silent fingers to Tom, saw him nod an affirmative, then shake his head at what his wife had just said. With that Lisa marched off inside the cabin to do what all I don't know. Whatever it was she had a purpose about her that nothing was going to stop, and as dangerous as the situation was I couldn't help but smile to myself. Lisa and Tally, they could be a couple of tough women when they wanted to be, and for that I was glad.

"Besides," I heard Lisa say from the darkness of the cabin, "she's my friend too."

There were three, maybe four hours of light left in the day when we saddled up. The men who had Tally only had three choices. They could ride for the desert, for the mountains, or for the tree lines that occasionally showed up at the base of the mountains. The high ground would have been the best choice to make a stand, but I was gambling that these outlaws were all pilgrims to this land and wouldn't know that. If a body got friendly enough with the Indians who lived in the mountains, he could find caves and hiding places in them that few white men had ever seen before or likely would. But this bunch likely hadn't been here that long and would avoid the Indians as much as they were trying to avoid us.

The desert was no match for any man who didn't know how to survive in it, and if I was right, these men knew better than to try it. At least half of those who had come to the gold fields had come across the desert in one form or another. The fiercest desert was the Mojave, for those who traveled the southern route and passed through Death Valley to get here. Others followed the South Pass that Jed Smith had opened in 1824 and on over the Sierra Madres to reach the gold fields. Either way, there were some long dry stretches, if a man didn't know where to look for water. No, the desert was out.

They had headed south, and it was those tree lines and the first bit of high ground that they clung to as we followed them until dusk. We weren't riding hell-for-leather, for I'd had enough jostling up of my insides for one week. This was a cat and mouse game we were playing now. They had someone who meant something to me, and they knew I'd come after her, knew I'd come after them.

You might say we were loaded for bear when it came to guns, and I'd not deny to anyone asking that I was on a hunting expedition, not at all. Each of us had two pistols, the second one stuck away inside our slickers, although Lisa had hers poked away in the saddle holster I'd designed for that massive Walker Pick Ax had used. I had my Hawken, Tom his sawed-off, and Dean the Colt's revolving shotgun. When he said he'd be riding shotgun I reckon he was serious about it.

We made camp in a thicket behind some rocks so as to hide our fire from sight. Lisa had cut some thick slices of bacon to fry up for that evening meal, as well as some biscuits that hadn't gotten old enough to harden yet to sop up the grease with. There was a smattering of beans and some coffee, and we made sure to enjoy it, for from there on out it was going to be hardtack and jerked beef and stale water.

There was a lot that could have been said for all that had taken place within the last week, but we pretty much ate in silence that night. I never did ask anyone else what was run-

ning through their mind, but I only had one thing on mine
and that was getting to these ruffians and maybe pulling
some of those Blackfoot bravado tests on them for openers.

One thing I'd found out about Americans in the time I'd
been roaming the West was that they tended to get right
moral and legal minded when things didn't go the way they
were supposed to. It was that way during the Mexican War
and hadn't changed since and likely never would. I did a
little thinking on that subject and made a fleeting comparison of our small group to the vigilance committees that were
being talked about. Ray Wallace would never tolerate them,
being the lawman that he was, for they were mob rule at best
with only one object in mind, and that was to make an example of a criminal so others would take heed. The way Ray
explained it, those vigilantes were more set on making an
example than they were on proving a man's innocence, and I
reckon he was right. I recall old Tom Jefferson saying something about it being more important that laws are carried out
right and proper than it is how they're written, and that
surely justified Ray's line of thought. But when you got out
in a country like this where the law was spread so thin that a
man *had* to be his own law at times, well, things changed.
And I reckon if you thought on it for a bit, the four of us
might have been just like those vigilantes Ray detested so
much. Except for one thing. The four of us were after justice
as much as any vigilante committee ever would be; it was
just that, as far as I was concerned, I had no use for making
an example of anyone. So far as we knew, there were only
eight of them, but I'll tell you, hoss, it wouldn't have mattered if there were a hundred. I don't know about the rest,
but I had no intention of letting a one of those bastards get
out of range of my sights alive! And if that was vigilanteism,
then so be it!!

The only thing that rattled me now was not knowing who
these yellow dogs were. Knowing a man's rep can give you
an edge, something you know about him that'll get him to
doing what he shouldn't ought to be doing. But I still
couldn't figure out who it was we were going up against or,

other than the fact that they had Tally and were using her to draw us into some kind of trap, why.

"You frown much harder, boy, and someone's likely to plant some corn in the furrows of your brow." It was Sam'l Dean doing the speaking. I reckon he was trying to make light of the situation, but I could tell that some of the life had left him, and unless I missed my guess, it was seeing Pick Ax gunned down that took it out of him. Life gets kind of hard for a while when you go through an experience like that; I know, for I'd been through it my own self.

"The planting I got in mind ain't got nothing to do with corn."

" 'Member that Poe fella?" he said, trying to be conversational.

"Yeah, why?"

"They's this story I read the other day of his, 'The Case of the Purloined Letter' it was. It's about this letter that gits stole, see? And the feller telling this story, why he has a friend figures out where it is while the police are tearing apart all sorts of rooms looking for hidden compartments. Only the letter was in plain sight all the time. It was just that nobody figured it to be that way." He paused a moment, wiping his forehead. "I'll tell you, lad, I don't know how much fifty thousand francs is, but it's gotta be more'n these fools digging out the river beds is making. That's what the fella got for his deee-tecting, you see?"

"Yeah, sure," I said, remembering the story. Then a thought hit me, and I started putting pieces of this puzzle together as though I knew exactly what the picture would look like.

"What's the matter, son? You look like you been struck by lightning."

"Could be, Sam'l, could be."

"You sure?"

"Sam'l, what ever happened to that banker who was giving Tally all the trouble when I was down there in New Orleans?" I asked, ignoring his comment.

"Oh, he's gone. I kept an eye on him all that time and you

can bet he was still keeping an interest in Tally, but he left 'bout six, eight months afore we did.''

"Just picked up and left?" It didn't sound right, not at all, for the man I was remembering was nothing like that. His type was too predictable in what they would do. And too crooked.

"Yup. Headed for new places, I ˙eckon. You know how that is. Man as shifty as him, why when he becomes known in one place he just natural leaves for another.''

Things were coming back to me now. There was the beating I had taken the first week I was in New Orleans. I'd never been able to prove it, but I was sure it had been that banker's men who had done it. And then there was the man who had entered the banker's office and gotten the drop on me as I was cussing out his boss. He would have done me in then and there if it hadn't been for Sam'l Dean sticking a real convincing gun in the man's back. I suddenly remembered his face, too. Names and places were coming back right quick to me now as I rose from the rock I sat on and poured some more coffee.

I always figured that habits were a bad thing to get into because a body got to taking things for granted then and that made you careless and forgetful at best. But things were starting to click some now, and it was looking like Tally and New Orleans and something from way back when was tied up in this whole adventure. One other piece fell in place then as I remembered the business card that Tom had shoved in my pocket after we'd first met Johnstone. Tom had said something about contacting one of his agents, and that's when a habit of mine paid off. I'd taken to collecting bits and pieces of paper and notes and such and shoving them into my shirt pocket. The thought of Johnstone made me go rumaging through my pocket until I found the calling card the express agent had left. And it explained a lot.

On the card was Johnstone's name and identity as an express agent for the Adams Express Company. And scrawled in Johnstone's barely legible handwriting underneath his name was the name of the man he had told Tom to contact if we got ready to sell our business to them. "*Wm. Esquire*" was what the agent had scribbled, and that, to me at least, explained a hell of a lot!

Bill was a nickname for William, and it was Bill who was the head of the highwaymen who'd been such a problem to us and to the stagecoach line in the past six months. I'd also bet money that it was Esquire who hired the woman to be there when Tally was around to embarrass me. But most important of all, I placed his name as the banker down in New Orleans who had given Tally all of her troubles when I'd first met her! And Sam'l Dean had just mentioned that the man had left six or eight months before he and Tally did, which would give him enough time to establish himself out here before she got here.

Suddenly there were a lot of things from the past that had an all too familiar bearing on the present. Too much had happened that had been passed off as coincidence that wasn't.

"Just what are you two getting at?" Tom asked, joining us.

"I think he's deee-tecting," Sam'l said, a bit of the mischief coming back to him.

"He's what?"

"Nothing, hoss," I said, returning to the present. "I just figured out who we're up against." When my partner only frowned in confusion, I said, "Look, Tom, remember that night we went drinking and got the hell beat out of us?"

"I'll say." It was likely one of those nights Tom wouldn't soon forget.

"Well, I remembered Ray saying we looked like we'd been shanghaied because there'd been some sort of net thrown over us."

"Yeah, so what?" Tom said, a confused look on his face.

"It just reminded me of a beating I'd taken down in New Orleans just after I'd met Tally. I never could prove it, but I always figured it was the work of a shady banker, Esquire. Now I know it was." I reached in my shirt pocket and pulled out one of the overly large gold pieces I'd found on the Rio Grande so long ago. "Remember Ray giving me this?" I held up the coin for inspection. "Said I must have dropped it?"

"Yeah."

"How many of these have you seen me use out here? None that I can recall. But I remember that a small sack full of 'em was stolen from me four years ago by those two men who beat me up in New Orleans. And I'm betting one of them dropped this coin when they did us in that night."

"Could be," Tom said, "but the sheriff's gonna think it's sorta thin evidence."

"Then what about those three outlaws we got this afternoon in front of our place? The one that Sam'l got was one of them who tried to hold us up the other day! No, Tom," I said shaking my head, "there's just too much coincidence for it to be any other way.

"What I figure is that Esquire set this whole thing up to get back at Tally and me." I looked at Lisa when I said, "And that he did."

"You think the woman was a set-up, too?" she asked, sipping her coffee.

"Had to be. She's just another coincidence that doesn't fit into the scheme of things. Besides, I just asked Sam'l and he said that Esquire left New Orleans about six or eight months before they did. And that fits right in with when Ray Wallace said the holdups started happening out here."

The conversation sort of dried up then, and Dean said he was going to check the horses. Lisa poured out the rest of the coffee and rinsed out the pot while Tom and I checked our loads. But I still had some questions on my mind that had gone unanswered in this whole affair. What was behind the stagecoach robberies I had no idea. The logical reason was money, but then the robbery that took place on the coach Tally was on didn't make any sense. Why take a trunk of clothing when a strongbox of money was available? Unless the robberies were just some sort of cover. I was putting the Dragoon back together when another thought struck me. What if Esquire thought Tally had something of importance in her trunk and knew that she'd be heading this way soon to join me? What if he'd convinced his gang that what he

wanted was the trunk and that they could have all of the
money in the strongboxes? Now that I thought of it, to hear
Ray Wallace talk, the holdups had been on stagecoaches
coming *to* Sacramento. That had to be it! There had to be
something in Tally's trunk, something she was bringing
west with her that had a value only to Esquire. But what? I
stuck the Dragoon back in its holster, and that was when I
knew what it was that was so important to Esquire.

That's also when I heard the click. It was a strong, hard
sound in the silence that made a chill run down my spine. It
was the cocking of a rifle, likely some heavy kind like my
Hawken . . . or one of those military rifles that had done in
Jory. We all heard it and all looked up at the man who stood
atop the rock some ten feet above us. You couldn't tell for
the beard on him, but I'd a notion he was ugly as sin the way
he was looking down that barrel. A man like that gets to enjoying his work too much and he winds up mean.

"Hold it right there, folks," he said, all business. "I'd
hate to think you're foolish enough to try something."

He had his sights on Tom, who stood off to his left. Lisa
was across the camp from Tom, and I had originally had my
back to the man. It was about that same time I remembered
that Dean had gone to check on the horses that we all heard
another click off in the darkness. It came from the far side of
camp, but it was only a split-second before the man on the
rock wheeled his long gun toward the sound.

He never made it. Before he could pull the trigger, the
Colt's shotgun let out a boom and the would-be killer flew
back against a rock, taking a full charge of buckshot in the
chest. If he wasn't dead when he hit the rock, I knew he was
when he rolled forward over and onto the log I'd been sitting
on.

"You're getting right handy at saving people's bacon,"
Tom said as we rolled the killer over on his back. Tom
studied the dead man's face while I picked up the rifle that
had fallen from his hands. It was a heavy old .50 caliber
army rifle that had been in use maybe ten years ago and
likely still was in most parts of the service. A gun like it had
killed Jory that morning; not this gun I was sure, for Ray

Wallace and his deputies would be upon us by now if it was and all I noticed then and there was how almighty quiet it had gotten.

Was there more than just the one killer? Had he been sent back to see if he could do us in alone? Or did he have friends out there in the night who'd make sure they wouldn't miss in case he did? Those questions went through my mind about then as I listened to the silence. It was the kind that can get on your nerves, that quiet. After you've been out here a while you get to noticing things; things like being on the prairie alone at night with nothing but you and the ground for a bed and the sky for a roof, and hearing Nature at work. There is the barely audible scuffle of prairie dogs scampering about. Or the hoot of an old owl if you're near some forestry and maybe even a bird or two calling it a night. And always the coyote. It's when you hear that *dead* silence that reminds you of the time you got your brave up to venture into a sure-enough graveyard on Halloween night and had the feeling there was life there you couldn't see; it's when Nature's elements have been scared away like that that you start getting real cautious.

"Know him?" Dean asked coming out of the shadows.

"Nope."

Lisa had seen enough blood since coming out here not to cringe at the sight of it, but I knew she had no use for flat-out killing and the wasting of life.

"Couldn't you have told him to drop his gun? To surrender?" she asked Dean.

"Young lady," he said, a stern look coming to his face, "you think about that question the next time you find you a snake what's been pestering you or a rat nibbles on your bread." It was going to be a long time before Sam'l Dean forgot about Pick Ax and what had happened to him, and I'd a hunch he wouldn't be at peace with anyone until the men who had been responsible for his friend's death got some sort of justice in the permanent fashion of lead. His voice got hard and there was a strong hatred in his eyes as he continued. "You don't give 'em second chances. You kill 'em on the spot! Lest you forgot already, he's one of the crowd that killed Pick Ax and damn near got you." His free arm shot out over her shoulder, pointing to the dead man. "Lady, that's snake meat."

I saw Lisa gulp hard when Dean walked back out into the darkness, almost as if he preferred it to the light of the campfire.

"I ain't seen him that fired up before," Tom said, watching the man go.

"I don't blame him," I said. "I felt the same way when Pa got killed."

"You got a special interest in him?" Tom asked when he saw me studying the dead man.

I nodded.

"He may be snake meat to Dean," I said to Tom, "but he's also gonna be the bait to pull in some more of those coyotes."

Chapter 13

The sky was clear, and the stars said it was midnight.

It had cooled off, but there was no breeze. I had given my buckskin jacket to Lisa, having spent enough nights in this kind of weather to be used to it. I had a notion that if I hadn't done that, given Lisa my jacket, she'd have gone to chattering with her teeth, she seemed that cold. And I didn't want anyone or anything giving us away.

The dead man was about Tom's size so we'd laid him out in Toms place and tossed a blanket over him and pulled his hat over his face as though he were sleeping. Our hats were all laid atop our saddles around the dying fire. If I was right and we got lucky, those bedrolls and deadwood under our blankets would lure some more of these vultures in for a second look. But then, I always figured most people make their own luck, so I reckon it was more a matter of whether they were fool enough to come in than it was any luck on our part.

I'd had Sam'l Dean hobble the horses, not wanting to prove how true the statement was that a man without a horse was nothing. These birds would want everything they could get their hands on, and it was Dean and his shotgun across the camp from us who'd make sure they didn't get it. I'd also warned him to fire *into* the camp rather than across it, for there was solid rock backing near the campfire and I'd no wish to have a ricocheting piece of buckshot put my eye out.

We sat there for three hours waiting. But while the rest of them were staring at the fire, wishing they could be near it, I was still trying to hash things out in my mind. I still had no idea as to what it was Esquire and his men could have wanted from Tally's trunk. All she said she had in it were a book or two for me and her clothes and personal things. But what could a woman have that a man like Esquire would want? It was still a man's world and men did all of the providing. Hell, even out in the gold fields a woman took to doing the woman's chores of a marriage while her husband mined for the gold. Gold. That last word stuck in my mind for a moment, trying to nudge something, almost as if it were the key to opening that locked drawer and all it needed was a good turn. I thought about it for a while and got nothing, so I thought about it some more and finally the key turned and that locked drawer was open. It was then I knew.

But by then it was midnight and at that instant it was time.

There were three of them this time. Two of them were big men, the third a short, stocky one. It always seemed sort of strange to me that the bigger a man got the more hardware he tended to pack with him. It was something to think about when I had the free time, but three hours of thinking had been enough for me that night. This wasn't the time for words or thought.

They said little as they began to fire their guns into the blankets as fast as they could. The body of the dead man moved when the bullets hit it, but the others only stirred up dust and a bunch of ricochets as they hit their targets. I reckon it was then they knew they'd walked into a trap. And that was when they were dead men.

One of them had stepped inside the camp and was about to turn to his side when Dean took him out with his shotgun, killing him the same way he had the first man. Tom shot the one in the center, killing him with his first shot, but the one closest to me broke and ran. I would have chanced a shot at him but he ran right in front of Tom. Any other time Tom would have reached out and grabbed him by the neck and yanked him back, but that shoulder wound of his must have been a bit rougher than he thought, for by the time he did reach out, he was just in the way. I broke and ran after the man myself, thankful that there was some sort of a moon out that night. He was fast and maybe thirty yards off when he tried to mount his horse. But I had the Dragoon trained on him as he pulled himself up over the saddle. His silhouette was outlined by the backdrop of the sky and that was when I fired. I aimed high but the shot struck him in the small of his back.

"He ain't going nowhere," I said when Tom came running out to me. I turned him over on his back and saw the youthful face of the man who had been about to kill me. "Ain't no more'n a kid."

"Helluva way to come into manhood," Tom said shaking his head. When he saw the look of remorse on my face he said, "Don't feel too bad, Finn. Someone would have got him not too far down the trail."

I nodded and we went back to camp, but I had a feeling then that I knew how Lisa must have felt about the waste of human life in all of this bloodshed. Now, hoss, I've read the Bible and all and heard men talk about wanting peace as much as a good homemade meal at times. But there's things you have to take into consideration, and one of them is that, after the class of people we'd been dealing with of late, why, you'd think the meek were going to get pushed off the end of this earth a long time before they had a chance at inheriting it, like the Good Book says. So I put the killing of that young lad out of my mind. We had things to do yet and I had a hunch we weren't through seeing our share of action.

"Are all three of them dead?" Lisa asked me as I returned to camp.

"Four," Dean said. Lisa gave him a hard, disgusted look and the old-timer said, "They was a feller out by the horses. He just got excited and . . . busted a blood vessel in his neck. Yeah, thass what happened to him."

I went out by the horses and found a fourth man dead, just as Dean said. But the blood vessel on his neck had been slit from ear to ear as a massive pool of blood formed around his head and shoulders. It was evident that Sam'l Dean wasn't playing any games; he was playing for keeps!

Nobody was going to be able to get much sleep the rest of the night anyway, so we moved on. We stripped the outlaws of their guns, powder, and ball and left them there. We turned all but one horse loose, setting them free, laying the saddles next to the bodies of the group of killers. Any remorse I had felt about killing the boy was gone at the sight of those outlaws, and I thought of how ruthlessly they would have killed all of us without so much as a blink of an eye.

There are signs a body can read in this country, signs left by humans and animals alike. I knew that the buzzards and coyotes would get to these bodies by sunup, but perhaps anyone who decided they wanted to raise hell in my territory again would have second thoughts when they looked upon the bones and saddles of these men. Sam'l, Tom, and Lisa tended to other things as I took to a chore of my own. I built up the fire and laid my bowie on the edge of it until it was good and hot. Using it as an iron, I fashioned a drawn-out S laid on the side of one of the saddles. In such a fashion it would look like a rattlesnake and, indeed, was a form of warning to those who knew the Spanish and Mexican traditions. *CUIDADO!* it said in Spanish, which, loosely translated meant, "Don't tread on me!" It was fair warning for any greedy sonofabitch who wasn't satisfied with making a living honestly; sort of let him know that he could wind up just like these gents. If you know what I mean.

It was only a couple of hours before daybreak, so we walked the horses until it looked as though first light was about ready to hatch a new day. Then we mounted up and picked up the outlaw's trail along the wood line, just like I figured. It only seemed logical, for what the horses couldn't forage for themselves in the way of grass, they could make up for with the bark of some trees, which served the same purpose.

The gunshots fired last night would have been heard for quite some distance, of that I was certain. I only hoped that if Esquire and his gang were anywhere within hearing range, they thought it was his men doing their job.

"Why did he send so many men after us?" Lisa asked.

"He had no way of knowing how many of us there were. Maybe he thought only you would come after him."

"Because men like Esquire don't like giving anybody an edge. Not ever," I said. "Besides, if he's as greedy as I remember him, he was likely trying to thin out his payroll and get me killed off to boot."

We trailed them for about an hour past sunup. The trail was yesterday's, yet it didn't seem as though they were trying to hide anything or cover their tracks. I reckon I'd been so worried about Tally's welfare that I wasn't thinking right just then. I should have known better, but I didn't.

Tom was talking about stopping for some water when we passed the edge of a rock formation that just opened up wide into a half canyon as soon as you came on it. It was a dead end and perfectly concealed from anyone not suspecting it, and I wasn't.

"Why don't you light and set a while, folks?"

He was big and unshaven and had a look about him that said he didn't give a damn. He stepped out from the mouth of that canyonlike entrance as easily as could be and stood in front of us at port arms, rifle at the ready. Tom and I were in the lead, and we were both going for our Colts when three more men sprang up from behind some rocks on higher ground. Each had a rifle and each was aimed directly at us. It was one of those situations where there wasn't much of a decision to be made.

Hoss, we were in trouble.

Chapter 14

That hole in the wall didn't lead back any more than a hundred yards, but it sure did open up some as we walked our mounts into it. Sort of a pear-shaped design is what it looked like; one entrance, one exit, both the same. It didn't seem too awfully smart an idea, but I reckon if you're only planning on staying a short time and moving on and the number of people who know about it are limited, well, then it might do. That may not seem like the right thing to be thinking about when you're looking down the business end of someone else's hardware, but as many tight spots as I'd been in of late, it was getting to be second nature.

The rifleman who'd met us at the entrance had been joined by two others from inside and had relieved us of our guns. Now we were walking our mounts inside, and I was hoping Tom was doing as much looking about as I was. I couldn't spot any other guards up in the rocks other than the original three who'd taken aim on us.

About halfway in I saw a semilivable shack about thirty yards off to the right. It surprised me actually to see a few trees inside this otherwise barren hole. The shack had been built near them, and I thought I saw Tally standing outside of it, two armed guards near her.

"I figured you'd come after me. But I didn't think you'd bring along your friends to die with you." It was Esquire. I'd recognize his voice in hell, no matter how hard I'd been trying to forget it! He was still cocky, still sneered at you when he spoke, still acted like he owned the world and everyone in it. I'd hated that about him from the first time I'd seen him four years ago. I'd stuck a foot out behind him and politely pushed him back over it, making a real fool out of him that first time, especially to all of those society people in that fancy New Orleans restaurant. And the sight of him just then made me think it hadn't ought to be any different the second time. I hit him as hard as I could on the jaw. Like I said, I'm tall and not as heavy as my brother, Nathan, but even he'll tell you that when the mad comes out of someone you don't expect, it can pack one hell of a wallop. And that's what it did to Esquire.

At the same time he went sprawling to the ground, I got run into from the left side and knocked off balance. I didn't fall, but I would have if Tom hadn't taken part of the blow. One of the guards on my left took a run at me, an arm full of guns and all, but Tom tripped him up and I only caught his shoulder as he fell against my lower leg.

"That's kinda dumb, friend," Tom said to the man as he got up. "Couldda got yourself and a few of us killed if those cannons started going off."

But it was Esquire I noticed as he got up, dusting himself off. I never did stick around to see what kind of damage I'd done to his hand after I'd brought that pistol of mine down on top of it four years ago, but from the looks it must have been considerable. I hadn't noticed it at first, but his right hand was held at his side as though it were sort of useless. What made it seem even more evident was the fact that the hand was encased in a thick, black glove. Now, I'm no doctor or anything, but it sure didn't seem like the nerves in his hand had much control over his fingers the way they twitched now.

"You'll regret that, Callahan," he said. I'd just gotten away with knocking him to the ground with his men present, but he had plans for me all along, of that I was sure. So the harshness of his voice didn't surprise me. He'd been a bitter man when I'd known him four years ago. Why should he change? Hell, maybe he was the only one of us who *hadn't* changed in the last four years!

"You're gonna die today, mister, and I'm gonna enjoy watching you die," Esquire said. Briefly, his left hand shot out and a hard finger punctured the air before me, as though to accentuate his meaning. "You ruined my reputation in New Orleans, then took the woman that could have been mine." Here he threw a harsh glance at me, then slowly began to work the thick, black glove from his right hand as he spoke. "But worst of all, Callahan, no man has the right to do what you did to me!" By then he had the glove off, and from the looks of those in view, including his own men, it was the first time he'd taken it from his hand. I was as shocked as the rest to see what now remained of his right hand. I distinctly remembered bringing down the butt of my pistol in the middle back of his hand, could see even now the look of horror that had formed on his face. But I had never thought I had done as much damage as I saw now. The thumb was the only movable part of the hand that was controlled by a muscle. The fingers moved involuntarily in the same nervous twitch I had seen at first. Other than that, they could have belonged to a man a hundred years old; a palsied hand with nothing but skin to cover the bare bones. Yet, as ogred as the hand looked, I felt no remorse for the man, for I knew the other side of the story.

"I never lost any sleep over anything I did to you, Esquire. You got just what was coming to you." I paused for a moment and let a mischievous smile come to my face so he wouldn't think he was the only one who could be cocky around here. "And you will yet."

He didn't like it one bit, my attitude, but when he stormed off I wasn't sure if it was the coward in him that kept him from doing something or if he had some special torture all worked out for me for later on.

We were escorted to where Tally sat atop her trunk of clothing. She didn't seem to look as uppity as she had when I'd left the day before. We had a long way to go, she and I, but I wasn't rushing into forgiveness right away. There was talking that had to be done and more than just a batch of clothes that needed to be ironed out. I wasn't sure whether to shake hands with her or take her in my arms, but when she looked up and saw us, saw me, I didn't have much choice. She came running at me full force, then must have remembered how bruised up I was because she slowed down some.

"Oh, Finn! I'm so glad to see you!" she said burying her head in my chest and grabbing hold of me like it was the first time. I slowly put my aching arms around her and gave her a hug of my own, freezing in my tracks as I did. When I backed away from her she was smiling, glad to see me, just like she said, but I had other things on my mind. I had noticed she was wearing that waistcoat I'd worn the night of the shindig. No wonder she looked drowned in it. I smiled at her then, but it was having felt the Baby Dragoon in the small of her back that made me grin.

"You are full of surprises, aren't you, girl?" I said in a low voice. The guards were some distance away and likely figured us for reunited lovers, and I'll tell you, friend, they could have been right. But just then I was feeling a good deal of pride in the gumption Tally had in her.

"I managed to sneak it into the back of my pants before they took me away," she replied in an equally low voice. "I told them I had to have a jacket because I was getting a cold and that's when I did it."

I raised my eyebrows in surprise and approval.

"You might have some bottom yet."

"That's not what you said the other night." All of a sudden we were talking like nothing had ever happened and this rock and a hard place we'd gotten into didn't exist. And, Tally being Tally, she was doing her best to make me laugh.

"Soon as you two get through introducing yourselves all over again, I figure we got some planning to do," Sam'l Dean said. He was back to acting the role of a cranky old-timer now and fully enjoying himself. Still, the man was right, we did have some coordinating to do if we were going to get out of here. One Baby Dragoon wasn't going to take out this whole gang, not if my count was right.

"I figure eight, maybe ten of 'em," Tom said, "if you count those three up on the rocks."

"Yeah," I said, "that's what I figure, too." To Tally I said, "Why'd Esquire come after you? Why'd he take you?"

"I don't know," she said and I could see that the mention of his name once again brought fear to her eyes. "He slapped me around some when he got me back here and started mumbling something about where all the gold was. I don't know what he was talking about."

"No, you wouldn't," I said, knowing it was the truth. I had her at a disadvantage then, and she looked at me as if some eye movement or contact would give her a hint as to what was going on. But Esquire and a couple of his men were heading toward us, so she'd have to find out for herself like the rest would.

"Now that I have you here, do you want to tell me where you've hidden it?" Esquire asked in that superior manner he had.

"Finn, what's he talking about?" Tally was the first to say it, then the others followed suit with the same question.

"I never had it hid, Esquire." I said it with a smile, letting him know I could deal a fair hand my own self. "If you wanted to know where it was, all you'd have had to do is ask."

"Finn, what in the hell's going on?" Tom never was one to be left in the dark on things; sort of ired him when things were that way. Like now.

I reached in my pocket and pulled out the oversized gold coin for all to see. "This is what our friend's interested in. Right, Esquire?"

"Yes." He didn't sound so cock sure now that what he thought was a secret was out.

"Root of all evil, I've heard it said." I flipped the coin and caught it, still smiling.

"To fools like you, yes, I suppose. But to me it's power and power is what controls the world. It always has and always will." He was real definite about that, but then I reckon most greedy men do share that philosophy. "Now, where is it?"

"On the banks of the Rio Grande," I said. "At a place called Resaca de la Palma."

"Don't play the fool with me, Callahan!"

"I'm not. That's the truth."

"No, it's not." He was an insistent cuss when it came to the subject of money, I'll say that. "I want the gold you've taken from these fields. Everyone's got their own little strike hidden away out here, Callahan, and I want yours, only I don't figure it'll be a little one. A man that had as much gold as you did in New Orleans, why, he'd know how to find that much and more in a place like this. *And I want it, now!*" The last was a demand.

"You're wrong, Esquire, that's not my style."

"He's right," Tom added. "I'd never have taken on a partner who had gold fever to work the business we're in." He shrugged. "You just hit a dry hole, hoss."

"You mean all of this was over the gold?" Tally said in amazement.

"It usually is out here," I said.

"I still don't understand," Lisa said.

"About four years back when I met Tally, I'd just come from two of the first battles of the Mexican War, Palo Alto and Resaca de la Palma. But before I rode to Orleans I came across a trunk full of more gold than I'd ever seen in my life. A couple of men died trying to take it from me. So I grabbed a saddlebag full of it and buried the rest. Figured I'd come back for it after the war was over.

"I had a lot of strange looks from people I tossed one of these to in that town, like they'd never seen anything like it before." Here I looked straight at Esquire. "Fact is, I got me ambushed and beat up there over what I was doing to help Tally. The fellas that did it used a *net* like some shanghaied sailor'd get on the Frisco waterfront"—Tom raised a knowing eyebrow as if he were catching on to the story—"and took a sack full of my gold coins for their trouble. I never could prove it, but I'm betting they were your men, Esquire."

"Touché." He forced a gentleman's smile.

"Say, thass real good deee-tective work, Finn," Dean

said. I could tell he was getting excited about the story, but I reckon reading Poe'll do that to a body.

"Same thing your Inspector Augustine would've done, Sam'l. Like he said, it was right out in the open. But first you've got to remember that Esquire here is a grudge fighter. He's not the kind to forget evening a score, no matter how small. Four years passed, and then by pure coincidence I sent for Tally about the same time his finances got low—or he got run out of town, one or the other. His men would have shown him that sack of gold of mine, so he likely figured that if he could intercept Tally on her way out here, he'd be able to find what he wanted, what he needed."

"And what was that?" Dean asked.

"That, Sam'l, was the purloined letter, just like Poe wrote about. Most women in love hang on to their love letters and Tally was no exception. If Esquire and his boys could get that trunk of hers, they'd be able to find something I'd told her about where my *gold mine* was located. And since he couldn't know which stage she'd be on, he and his men hit everyone that came west. And if Tally and the trunk weren't on it"—here I shrugged—"they could at least get the strong box or a payroll to make it worth their while."

"What about the girl?" Lisa asked. "The one in town those two times?"

"She was part of the plan to tear Finn and me apart," Tally said, and now it was I who was surprised. "Both times she looked familiar to me, but I couldn't place her. I made the mistake of thinking she was the other woman in Finn's life. But when they brought me here last night I knew for sure what had happened." She got real humble all of a sudden as she looked up at me. "She was wearing my dress that second time, and I was so jealous that I didn't even notice it." Then in a softer voice, as though no one else would hear her, she added, "I was such a fool." But any romantic feelings she might have had soon faded as she turned to Esquire. Or maybe they were just starting as she continued. "Finn never wrote me about his gold, Mr. Esquire. I knew of it, yes, but I didn't care about it then, nor do I care about it now. He's worth more to me than all the money you'll ever lay your hands on in your lifetime." I took her hand and squeezed it, hoping that she'd know how proud I was feeling of her right then. This was the Tally I knew back in '46. Yep, that was my girl.

"I went back after the war, or at least my part of it, was over, Esquire," I said. "Dug up that trunk of gold and damn near lost my life doing it. There never was a gold mine, friend, and a good share of what I first had is gone now, so you're wasting your time with us. Now, what say you just turn us loose and you go your way and we'll go ours?"

Using logic like that against three-to-one odds doesn't seem all that sane, I reckon, but I thought it might be worth a try. What I got was a few chuckles from Esquire.

"You're offering *me* a deal? Don't make me laugh, Callahan."

"Well, now, if you think about it, it does make some kind of sense," Dean said, trying to sound enthusiastic. "We's just gonna go 'bout our business and you'd have a chance to get outta the territory."

"Not a chance, old man. *You* might make such a deal, but your friend here, Callahan, he's a different matter." He was silent a moment and I could see the wheels turning inside his mind. "Besides, I don't like witnesses." Silence again, more wheels turning. Then he turned to one of the guards. "Tell the boys to get their gear, we're leaving." When the man left, the other guard frowned at his boss.

"What about them?"

"Pack your gear and kill 'em . . . ALL of them!"

Like I said, Esquire was a grudge fighter, and people like that figure to have their way in the end. He walked off with a confident look on his face, a man fully in charge.

"Sam'l," Tom said, "I don't suppose those Blackfeet taught you how to get out of a tight spot, did they?"

"Nope," the old-timer said matter of factly. "Learned all by myself on that one. Yup, surely did."

"And what's that?"

"Why, fight our way out!" he said in that flabbergasted way an old-timer has of letting you know something he figures ought to be common knowledge by now. Luckily, he said it low enough so that it wouldn't attract any attention. "Any mountain man worth his salt that seed Ezekiel a-coming, why he'd fight it out, he would."

"I don't see how we're gonna get too awful far with what we ain't got," Tom said.

"Do like the man says, Tom," I said, an idea striking me, "we'll fight our way out. Look, we get these two guards, we can take their guns and keep going from there—"

"—and hope everyone else we come across ain't used up all their ammunition shooting us full of holes. Damn, but you play the long shot, Finn!"

"You keep underestimating the power of a woman," Tally said with a smile.

"I keep hearing that," Tom said, sounding as though he were getting tired of it.

"Oh, she's got a surprise all right, Tom," I said, forgetting that I'd not told anyone about the Baby Dragoon in the small of Tally's back.

"Gentlemen, how soon do you want to get out of here?" she asked.

"The sooner the better," Tom said and Sam'l Dean and I nodded.

"Then please indulge me in a bit of play acting," Tally said, and tugged at my arm, pulling me toward her trunk.

She opened it and began to rummage around in it, pushing her dresses and things around until she found what she wanted. I was surprised that the guard didn't pay closer attention to what she was doing.

"They went through my trunk," she said in a low voice as she continued to look around. "Apparently, the ones who did it aren't much for reading and thank God for that. Oh, here they are." She pulled out two books, balancing an oversized third one on the corner of the trunk. Then, in a sincere voice she seemed to once again forget the danger of the moment as the softness returned to her eyes and she said, "These were to be my present to you. One of them is the third volume of Bancroft's *History of the United States* you said you couldn't find. The other is a new book by a Nathaniel Hawthorne, *The Scarlet Letter*. Ironically, it's about hypocrisy in New England.'' A tear came to her eye as she paused a moment. ''I suppose there's a lot to be learned by both of us from that one.'' She set the books back in the trunk and took my hand in hers. ''I just wanted you to know that if something happens and . . . I just want you to know how very much I love you right now. How very much.''

''I know,'' I said getting a knot in my stomach. ''You ain't alone in that feeling. It's a helluva way to be coming to an understanding though.''

''Yes,'' she smiled, wiping away the tear. ''Well, now let me show you my real surprise.'' She stood up grasping the big book on corner of her trunk, holding it in one hand while she once again guided me, this time away from the group. She stopped when I was more out in the open, where more people could see us. I saw her glance off to the side then and did so myself, catching sight of that blond woman who had caused all the trouble in town for me. She had on another of Tally's fancy outfits from back in New Orleans, one that I remembered. Then Tally thrust the book into my hands.

A lot of the bigger books in those days where thick and bulky, and sometimes the only way you could tell how expensive they were was by the cover. This one was brand new and a couple, maybe three inches thick. The leather binding on it was of a fine quality and for a minute I thought it might be something new by Dickens, since he tended toward bigger novels.

''I told Sam how I knew you, and he made it special for me to give to you,'' Tally said, a hint of mischief coming to her eye. Here we were about to get killed, and she was funning about it!

''Sam?'' I frowned, ''I don't know no author name of Sam.'' Then I opéned the book and got the surprise of my life as I did my damnedest to stay calm. I closed the cover quick and looked at the binding on the back of the book. ''I should have known,'' I said, slowly shaking my head in disbelief. ''You got a surprise or two left in you, woman, that you do.''

The title of the book read *Colt's Companion* and inside

was, you guessed it, a Baby Dragoon. It had those fancy swirly-gigs engraved on the cylinder and sides of the pistol and a fine pair of shiny wooden stocks. Leave it to Sam Colt, I thought to myself, to go first-class all the way. He was getting a reputation for making gifts of fancy pistols like this to every foreign dignitary who came to America and doing it in his own way. Me, I'd known Sam from back when we were kids in Hartford and he got farmed out to a place near ours for a year or two. My brother and I were that close to Sam Colt, and there were times I didn't think he'd find any better agents for selling his weaponry than we Callahans. I reckon I should have known that Sam, knowing I liked to read, would fix up something like this for me, but the sight of it threw me and I felt a wave of surprise and relief pass over me at the same time then. Surprise at seeing another pistol made available to us, and relief in the knowledge that with it we had a chance of lowering the odds considerably.

"I told Sam you'd like it."

"Right now I can't think of a more appropriate present."

She gave me a peck on the check, then a brief smile.

"Now, run your hand up my side and give the look you had on your face that first night I got here."

Now, hoss, there's some things a man just naturally keeps private to himself and those kind of thoughts are one of them. But the lady seemed to be running the show and this seemed to be a day of surprises, so I did as she requested. Besides, there comes a time when you forget about the odds you're playing, especially when they're as steep as the ones we were bucking, and just say to hell with it.

I don't mind telling you that I forgot about what I was thinking right quick, for that was when Tally swung the flat of her hand up against my face and I'd have bet all the gold in that valley of ours that the ringing inside my head was as loud as the echo that slap made! If it was shock effect she was looking for, by God she got it!

"How dare you!" she yelled out loud, enough for the whole camp to hear. She had a look on her that was meaner than hell, and without waiting for my reaction she ran to

Tom, who stood a few yards away, throwing her arms around him. And you know, I think that shocked him as much as it did me.

"Oh, Tom, it was you I wanted all along! Please help me!" She said it all loud enough for all to hear, but I was betting it was Lisa who was shocked the most. The poor woman was turning as red a shade as the last barn I'd painted and was getting that look all women who've been betrayed get when they find out—she was ready to kill! But Tally paid no attention to her and buried her head in Tom's chest as we all watched. She must have said something, for it was only a second or two later that Tom put his arms around her and was patting her on the back with one hand while he moved the other under my waistcoat she was wearing and stopped. Then he looked at me and gave a slight nod of the head and I knew. I knew he had his hand on that Baby Dragoon Tally had managed to conceal in the small of her back. Yes, she'd do to ride the river with, that Tally!

"Ouch!" Sam'l Dean put his hand up to his neck, rubbing it as though it had a cramp in it.

"Careful, old man," the guard said.

"Well, what do you expect, you young pup! Wait'll you get old as me and your bones'll be able to tell you all sorts of things 'bout the weather." He kept rubbing, glanced up at the sky, which had begun to cloud a bit, then over to me. "Gonna rain, Finn," was all he said. "Any minute now." That might have been a forecast, but it had little to do with the weather if I was reading it the way he meant it. The rain would be large doses of lead.

In a way it only seemed fitting that Sam'l Dean open the ball, for it was he who had come for vengeance. I'd come to get Tally, and Tom and Lisa, well, I reckon they came because they wouldn't have had it any other way.

Sam'l reached a bit further down the back of his neck than before and in one motion brought out a scaled down version of a Green River knife that most mountain men used. It was his ace in the hole, and he put it to good use. In one motion he threw it into the guard's chest, the one who had been standing not far from where our weapons were piled.

"Now, Finn!" Tom yelled, pushing Tally away as he brought his Dragoon around and shot the guard nearest him.

At the same time I pulled my own Dragoon out of that book and put an end to the life of that guard Sam'l had knifed. I whirled and shot the one not too far from me and grabbed his pistol, an old Walker-Paterson, as he fell to the ground. I started shooting like there was no tomorrow then, and the truth of the matter was that if I hadn't, well, damn it, there wouldn't be any tomorrow!

People started coming out of everywhere just then! Sam'l had picked up his Colt's shotgun and scared a few chargers away with a sprinkling of his buckshot. Then I saw him fall forward, shot in the back. At first I didn't know where it had come from, for we as good as had our backs to the wall. Then I remembered the lookouts up in the rocks. I spotted the one who must have done the shooting and tossed the Colt's on a dead guard's chest for an instant as I grabbed up his rifle and took aim at the man who brazenly stood in plain view as he reloaded his own weapon. At its fastest, it'll take a man twenty seconds to reload a musket or rifle and that was all the time I needed. He was a good seventy-five yards off, but the rifle was true, and he was dead before his body fell the fifty-some feet to the ground below.

A split-second later I felt my left leg being kicked out from under me. As I fell I saw Esquire standing to my left, cocking his pistol to do me in for good. But a shot roared to my rear, and when I looked back there was Tally, holding a Colt in both hands. There's just so much hatred you can put in a person's eyes, and she had it all right then as she watched Esquire clutch a hand to his chest before he fell dead. Whatever it was that had been bothering Tally about him died the instant he hit the ground. When I looked back, she stuck a hand out to me and gave me some help getting back on my feet, then planted the Colt in my hand.

"Here," she said, oblivious to my presence. "I've got some other business to take care of."

Indeed she did, for she set out at a run, cussing a blue streak like I'd never heard from a woman, but then, this was no society ball either. She charged right at that blond woman, giving her a whack across the nose and dragging her down to the ground. It wasn't but a second later that Lisa ran by me and joined in the fandango that was taking place.

Tom was holding his own as he helped Sam'l to his feet. That old man sure had a lot left in him, right up to the end. I yelled "Look out!" but it was too late as one of the outlaws came running at Tom with a bowie in his hand. That was when Sam'l stepped in front of Tom and brought that shotgun of his up into the man's belly as the bowie sank into his own. The blast of the shotgun knocked both of them back, Sam'l falling to the ground again while the outlaw sort of fell in half as most of his middle went flying off here and there in little pieces.

I was right about this gang, they were all a bunch of coyotes! The four or so left had taken note of Esquire's body lying motionless in front of that shack and thought better of attacking what must have seemed like three madmen. They grabbed what mounts they could find and headed for the mouth of the pear-shaped canyon. For now, it seemed, the battle was over.

I hobbled over to where Tom had just pulled the knife out of Sam'ls belly. There had been blood all over his back when he was standing, but the pool beneath him was widening now and it wouldn't be long before he was dead.

"Told you you'd need someone riding shotgun for you," he muttered to Tom.

"Never had a better one, Sam'l, never better." The way he was talking I got the impression that Tom had taken a liking to this old reprobate too.

"Finn."

"Yeah, Sam'l." It pained me to kneel down, but I did it. I reckon there were a lot of us who'd taken a liking to Sam'l Dean and maybe didn't admit it.

He tried to grin, but it was a seriousness that came to his face when he spoke.

"You stay outta trouble, boy . . . and take care of Tally. She ain't got nobody . . . now."

"Yes, she does, Sam'l," I vowed, "yes, she does." But his head sank to the side, and I could only hope that he'd heard those last words.

"Did you mean that, Finn? Did you *really* mean it?"

In back of me stood Tally, a few scratches on her face, tears rolling down her cheeks. I struggled to get to my feet but made it as Tom gave me a hand.

"Yes, Tally," I said, looking into her dark eyes. "I meant it, every word of it."

She rushed into my arms, holding me tight, and for that one instant I forgot about the death that surrounded us. But that instant was short lived.

Two shots rang out, both from a distance. Nothing came our way, and Tom gave me a curious glance, likely wondering the same thing running through my mind. What in the hell was going on now? That answer was soon apparent as a volley of shots that sounded even more distant were fired and one of the guards atop the rock formation jumped back two or three times as though he'd been hit by as many different shots. As it turned out, he had.

That was when those banditos making their escape did an about face and headed right back toward us! I don't think any of us knew what was taking place, only that there were five desperate men riding hell-for-leather in our direction! At the moment they were out of handgun range, but another shot rang out from the ridge as Tom spun around and once again the rifleman had hit his mark.

"Are you all right?" Lisa said rushing to her husband's side. But it was only a flesh wound and not in Tom's shooting arm.

"Gimme that Hawken," he growled, sitting up and ignoring his wife. "I'm gonna blow that sonofabitch from here to kingdom come."

I tossed the long gun to him, trusting that he was mad enough to carry out his threat before turning back to the horsemen charging our way. There was no time to reload, so

I made my way to the Colts I'd left on the dead man, for they were the only guns I was certain still contained loads. It was then that I thought I knew what had happened, for not far behind those men riding toward us my eye caught glint of light from more horsemen. By God, it was Ray Wallace and his deputies!

"Nathan said he wanted a woman who'd stand beside him and not behind him," I said, handing one of the pistols to Tally. "You feel up to it?"

I heard the Hawken boom then, and out of the corner of my eye saw the last lookout fall from the rocks. It was then the horsemen got into range and Tally gave her answer.

She fired twice in succession, knocking the first horseman out of the saddle and killing the second horse, sending its rider head over heels as both rolled on the ground. I could feel the lead flying past me then as I took aim and shot one man out of the saddle. One of Ray's men must have got the fella on the right, for he fell from the saddle too.

That fella who'd taken the spill from Tally's shot must have been feeling awful mean about it, for the horse just missed him when they hit the ground, and he was up in an instant, rushing toward Tally. She fired her pistol twice, but it misfired both times. Then she threw the gun at the outlaw who had now drawn his knife, having lost his own pistol. He might have been within six feet of her when I fired my last shot. But I could only hope I'd killed him, for the last horseman was upon me then, jumping me from his mount. If he wasn't two hundred pounds, he sure felt like it when he landed on top of me, knocking the air out of me and nearly knocking me unconscious. He was sitting atop my chest now and he, too, had a knife drawn. He was uglier than Pick Ax could ever have been, but I couldn't think of anything else to do. I was about to die, and the only thing I had the strength to do was spit in his face and hope I died with a defiant look on my face to match the way I felt. The spit took him by surprise but did not stop him as he swung his arm in an arch to bring the blade in and slit my throat.

Then over his shoulder I saw Ray Wallace on his horse and a shot rang out and the man's body was forced down on top of mine as I passed out.

Chapter 15

They say it was a week before I came to. Loss of blood and infection and all sorts of medical terms that Lisa spouted off to me. But it was Tally's face I first saw when I woke up.

"You're a pretty tough man, Callahan," she said with that engaging smile she had. It took a minute to remember where I was and what had happened, but she didn't want to talk about it, instead feeding me some soup. I drifted off to sleep, and she came back a while later and this time we talked some.

"Your friend, the sheriff, saved your life," she said.

"Yeah," I said weakly, remembering that part of it. "I know." Then I recalled the man who'd charged Tally and asked her about him.

"He died right where you shot him. They captured one. The rest are dead." She paused a moment and her eyes got kind of sad looking. "We buried Sam'l Dean next to Pick Ax. Tom said he'd have wanted it that way."

"Yeah."

"Oh, Finn, it's so good to have you back." She was crying then and kissing me and holding on to whatever part of me hadn't been bandaged up, but what little it was felt good. Damn good.

The wedding took place two weeks later. Tally and Lisa claimed it would take a woman at least that much time to

161

find the right materials and make the necessary dresses for the occasion. That's what they said, but I figured it was likely they were giving me the time to recover and be able to get around on that day.

Tom managed to get most of the runs made by himself during that time, but after the first week I was up and using a cane to get around and help with the livestock and such as I could.

Somehow, Tally and I never did get around to all of that talking I figured was needed, maybe because what we had said and did for each other out in that canyon had been enough to make us both understand the meaning of love. Still, I had to laugh at Tom and the advice he kept giving me on how to handle women. I ignored a good share of it, basically because I'd seen the way he handled women and figured he did a better job with horses. But I wasn't about to dash his hopes on giving sound advice.

I was pretty well recovered by the day of the wedding. I had a limp and my side was still stiff, but I knew where I was and what I was doing and that was what counted.

We had the ceremony down in the valley instead of in one of the fancy churches in Sacramento. The padre said he didn't care where it took place, so we had it down there. That way all of those miners didn't have to go too far to attend. After all, it was they who had trusted Tom and me with having enough integrity and honor to get their gold to the assayer's office in Sacramento, and it's friends like that that you want to have around for special occasions like this.

I think every one of those miners took himself a turn at kissing the bride after the ceremony was over, so I spent some time with Johnstone, the Adams Express agent who'd made the trip for the ceremony and apologized to him for what I'd done to him. He was good enough to forget the whole thing, but I was still curious about one thing.

"How come you hesitated like you did when I asked you your middle name?"

"Probably because I don't have one," he said turning just a light shade of pink. "My parents were argumentative, I suppose, so I wound up with an initial instead of a full name. It's been a sore spot of mine for most of my life."

When he asked me if I had changed my mind about selling out to Adams, I said no, that Tom and I would continue doing our own business.

"Besides, Sam'l Dean mentioned one time that there was a fella down Santa Fe who might be willing to look into a partnership with us. Alexander Majors I think he said his name was."

"Oh, yes," he said, obviously aware of the man. "I've heard some good things about him. He's getting quite a reputation as a dependable freighting man." And that closed the subject.

I'd been to my brother's wedding back in '36 when he married Ellie Harper. And I'd been to Tom and Lisa's wedding in '47 after we got back from the Mexican War. But this one was the best; maybe because it was mine. I didn't do an awful lot of dancing, but you can bet this shindig was one to beat that first one we'd had for Tally when she arrived out here. There was a good time had by all and sort of a general holiday spirit to the whole day's events. It was toward sundown that Tom borrowed Johnstone's buckboard and gave us a ride back up to the cabin. Old Tom, he wasn't feeling too bad about then, not bad at all.

"Want a drink, Finn?" he asked as Tally and I got out of the buckboard. She had worn a flowing white dress that must have had I don't know how many petticoats, but I don't think there was a miner that afternoon whom she hadn't turned an ankle for. She was a real beauty, this one. And all mine.

"No thanks, Tom," I said with a smile. "I think this is one night I want to remember." I was looking at Tally when I said it, and she blushed.

"Sure you do." He eyed Tally up and down, then looked back at me. "And you will, too. You will."

Then he was gone.

I did remember that night, still do. But it was during the night that I recalled something Pa had told us boys when we were youngsters. I didn't understand it until just then. He said, "Boys, when you find the woman you want to spend your life with, hang on to your hat 'cause it's one helluva ride!"

And you know, hoss, he was right!

Author's Note

Aside from being the first express company to see the advantages of setting up a headquarters in the California Territory—which it did in December of 1849—the Adams Express Company was the most prestigious of those that ventured into the express business. It bought out a number of its smaller competitors during the heyday of the Gold Rush, but a depressed economy in 1854 in the East led to many of the businesses in California closing down for a short time in February 1855, and although its toughest competitor, Wells, Fargo & Company, was found to be solvent, the Adams Express Company did not reopen and was put into receivership. However, it did play an important role in the Civil War, along with the Southern Express, both being known as the only express companies to provide feasible lines of communication for passengers and mail between the North and the South.

The Adams Express Company never did enjoy the fame, glory, and publicity that the Wells, Fargo Company did, but it did play an important part in pioneering the express business as this country continued to grow in the mid-nineteenth century, and for that it deserves more than just a casual mention.

Alvin Adams, who founded it in 1840 in Massachusetts, and was its president for fifteen years, had a lot to be proud of.

Jim Miller

About the Author

Jim Miller began his writing career at age ten when his uncle presented him with his first Zane Grey novel. A direct descendant of Leif Erickson and Eric the Red, and a thirteen-year army veteran, Mr. Miller boasts that stories of adventure flow naturally in his blood. His novels to date include SUNSETS, GONE TO TEXAS, COMANCHE TRAIL and WAR CLOUDS.

When not busy writing about the future exploits of the Callahan brothers, Mr. Miller spends his time ensconced in his 2,000-volume library filled mostly with history and research texts on the Old West.

Mr. Miller lives in Aurora, Colorado with his wife and their two children.